The Realtor
(Under Construction)

DANA L. KLEIN

DKMC, Inc.
PO Box 222094
Hollywood, FL 33022

First Edition

Cover art and design by Tom Korba
www.southbeachgraffix.com

Library of Congress Control Number: 2016906215

While some stories use real place names, settings, and historical facts, this book is a complete work of fiction. Any resemblances to actual events or persons, living or dead, are meant to be resemblances and not actual representations of events or persons, living or dead.

Printed on acid-free paper
ISBN   9780997502404
ISBN: 0997502401

DEDICATION

To my beloved parents Rubin and Abbey as well as my grandmother the infamous fashion editor Ruth Peskin (aka Ruth Preston). I hope they are resting in peace and not getting angina from all they are witnessing from their vantage point.
I am so very grateful to have known and loved them. They taught me lessons and protected me. No matter how old I get, they will always be smarter than me.
Thank you.

ACKNOWLEDGEMENTS

Thank you Martha, Nicole, and Rachel Peskin, Barbara Daelman, Vin DiBona, Steven and Sandra Colyer, Jill Kovalich, Jennifer Pierce, Abraham Fischler, Tomas Abreu, Cami Green, Gligor Tashkovich, Bill Miller, Alan Cohen, and Diane Brennan for all your encouragement and support in writing this book.

My editor Barbara London, thank you, thank you, thank you!

To Karen Fraser because she's my idol.

Ben Franklin for his lessons and diplomacy we all should abide by but probably never will. He's a tough act to follow.

My broker Juan Baixeras for instilling a sense of humor in the workplace and bailing me out of trouble all the time.

Emerson College and Syracuse University who taught me how to read, write, and create. It was expensive but hopefully well worth it.

South Florida for all its blessed fodder.

To me and to you because that's what it's all about, well, primarily me. We must all know our place.

To all the careers I've loved before,
May I be broke never more.

1

Lena Gorman sat up in bed, put her hands on her chest, and cried out "Oh my God. My boobs! Where are they? I'm 49 and I don't know where my boobs are!"

The bed was a gift from her father when she first moved into her townhouse. He said she could buy any bed in the store she wanted. She reviewed several options over the course of an hour and picked the one she liked. He bought her the cheapest one in the store instead. It was part of a two-for-one special. Her sister got the other one and upgraded it quietly before delivery.

She lifted her eye mask, looked around and surveyed the room. It was a myriad of contradictions with antiques and new collectibles. It was also a mess. It was a mess in a cookie-cutter townhouse in a cookie-cutter complex she never thought she'd live in. What if she were to die here?

Lena lived in a neighborhood where old men in cars replaced boys on bikes delivering morning newspapers. Where intelligent, grown people picked up after their dogs who led them rigorously down the street attracted to every scent and distraction. Where drivers ferociously drove from one block to the next, coming to skidding halts at frequently placed stop signs.

Lena looked across the room at the mirror in the corner. She was a scary sight. Strategically, she maneuvered out of bed, adjusted the clothes on the floor into a bigger pile, stepped over it, and exited the room.

She descended the stairs slowly making her way toward the kitchen to begin her day, her daily routine, the assembly line of her life. She took hold of the electronic teapot, poured in water, hit the button to boil, grabbed a mug, added a teabag, stared at the pot, and waited. Last year she gave up coffee to be more relaxed and patient for the benefit of those around her. All it did was frustrate her further.

After a moment, she took the oatmeal out of the cupboard and waited some more. The teapot clicked off. She poured the boiling water into the usual mug and bowl. She steeped the teabag and stirred the oatmeal. Though her ritual was only 90 seconds long, it felt more like half an hour. Her morning mind simply digested things more slowly these days.

Middle aged and confused, Lena grew up as part of Gen X, with too many choices and time to indulge. She was bored by the treadmill of her own life and regretted not doing, giving, and being more to the world either personally or professionally. Though moderately successful, she felt unaccomplished and unsatisfied. She never married nor had children, though she always expected she would. Somehow, she had missed the boat on everything. She should have been more like her father, focusing on priorities and the big picture. And yet, she knew she had a wonderful life compared to most and hoped and believed the best was still yet to come. This really couldn't be it for her.

She needed some direction. She decided to set up an appointment with her psychic. But it was touch and go. Since the psychic's recent head injury, she would either read in a deep trance or be totally out of it. Still, Lena liked listening to psychic Joan because the conversation was always all about her.

2

Mind, body, and soul continued to wake up, prepare for the day, and get ready for work. She climbed back upstairs in all her morning glory, sauntered into the bathroom to brush her teeth and examined herself in the mirror. Lena looked young for her age and wondered how that happened. Certainly nothing she did could have helped. Perhaps it was because she never had children.

As she brushed, lather congregated around her mouth. She spat and smiled at the mirror. She hoped positive feelings would back her thoughts and intentions throughout the day. She was not really a perky and happy specimen to begin with and had to work at it.

This morning she was a little more sluggish than usual. The night before, she was in charge of the Prince of Monaco's protocol for his visit to South Florida. Since Lena had already been working with the event's sponsor, and this was a ceremony that required special VIP services and public relations, she was the easy choice. It's what she did for a living. She made all the arrangements for the honoree's arrival, participation, and departure. When the prince arrived, he was properly escorted to and from the airport, and to and from his hotel.

The most challenging problem she had preparing for the visit was the wardrobe, not his, hers. She had to make serious choices on what to wear. She couldn't decide which bra would work with her backless dress, so she brought two of them to the function. Her perfectly matched shoes were slightly too big, so she stuffed them with toilet paper. Ten minutes before the prince arrived, Lena was perfectly situated in her dress, boobs secured, and shoes on tight, and raring to go.

Wrapped in a sash, the prince walked up to the door with his bodyguard in tow.

"Are you the one that takes care of me from here?" he inquired in a voice as smooth as satin.

"Yes Your Majesty," was all Lena could manage to spit out.

He put his hand on her back and said "Lead me to my seat." Lena melted. In fact, she almost fainted. "Oh my God, Oh my God, Oh my God," she said under her breath as she led the way. He was so debonair. As she led him to the front of the room, her bra strap slid down her arm and toilet paper unraveled out of her shoes. She tried to adjust without bringing distraction. It was a full body struggle. Finally, they arrived at the table.

"Your Majesty," she said as she guided him into his seat. "Should you need anything else, I'll be waiting in the wings."

"You're wonderful," he replied.

Lena smiled awkwardly and exited towards the darkened side of the room out of the limelight. "Oh my God, oh my God, oh my God," she continued to say to herself.

Her friend Susan joined her from the shadows. Susan was a practical looking, sensibly dressed woman of the same age. She was the type that did everything right, expected others to do the same, and took no chances. She was Lena's closest friend from early on who reminded Lena about herself. She counter balanced Lena and allowed her plenty of talk time to work things through while she provided insightful advice. Though Susan came from a similar background, they took different paths of employment and the perspectives were telling. Both being middle aged, they often used a form of charades and mad libs to communicate when certain words failed them, an activity that didn't help in the quest for work in the marketing communications industries.

"By Jove, I think she's got it," said Susan.

"Dear God. Please make this fantastic moment be over soon," said Lena.

"I can't believe you're doing the protocol for the prince. I have it all on video to be released on...you know...shortly." Susan was stuck on the words and used her arms for clarification.

"YouTube," Lena sighed. "What a true prince. I was an easy pick. I'm better behind the scenes."

"Yes, image is everything." Susan looked Lena up and down. "Speaking of which, what's up with yours? You're like...unraveling. You can't seem to fill your own shoes. Or your bra, apparently."

As everyone prepared to leave after the program, the prince mistakenly found Lena's box of supplies with her extra bra inside. She was mortified. He smiled. She didn't dare move or say anything. She would have fainted for sure.

The prince was just that, a prince. He thanked her for her good work. To show his appreciation, he gave her a scarf package with the words, "from the Palace of Monaco" printed on the ribbon. She sighed, letting out the deep breath she had been holding for a dangerously long time.

At home, Lena placed the package on the dresser all by itself in her messy bedroom. She had no clue what was in it but didn't want to ruin the ribbon or the memory of the moment. She would continue to stare at it lovingly every day from then on.

3

Time to make the big trip from bedroom suite to home office two doors down. The office walls were lined with diplomas, accolades, and photos of Lena with politicians, diplomats, and actors. Advertising with edits, marketing materials, notes on interviews, etc. lay about. Books such as "The Art of War" by Sun Tzu and Zig Ziglar's "Selling 101" sat on a shelf. A framed dollar bill hung over her computer.

Lena moved a cat off her chair and another off the desk. She sat at the computer and began her work. The short commute was a bit anticlimactic. What would it be like to go back to sitting in South Florida traffic for two hours a day? Steamy, she imagined. Perish the thought.

There had been an office downtown at one point, but no one came to it. In order to be more efficient with her resources, she closed it. The business was revamped as an outsourced commodity, and her employees were put on per project contracts. She took advantage of the time and money she saved on traffic and overhead to build her business. Traffic time was replaced with extensive proposal writing, customer service, and networking. Her successful home-based boutique firm ran mostly on old-fashioned hard work and spit, polish, and shine. The quality improved, expenses dropped, and things moved along as well as they should. Having no other diversions or assistants kept her focused and more involved on what she actually did for a living.

The past 20 years had been an interesting ride with lots of hard work. She had made money, had flat years, and always paid her bills. Whatever the situation, Lena always made a point to appear cool, collected, and sophisticated. She wore suits and perfectly matched accessories along with control top pantyhose and appropriate, sometimes ill-fitting and uncomfortable shoes. She was always meticulously prepared, coiffed, and in control. Sometimes she caused angst amongst her competition or jealousy from her colleagues, making things just a little rougher around the edges. But it always worked out. And she knew they would feel better if they saw the state of her living quarters.

Making service and quality top priorities as a small business owner posed a trap that was both difficult to control and unavoidable for her competitive edge. Clients knew it. They loved small businesses because of it. Lena continuously struggled to balance the "time is money" thing with her high standards of good old-fashioned service and exceptional quality even when unexpected. Most of the time, the extra effort went unappreciated. There were also no boundaries when it came to helping others, and she often put herself at risk to do so. She found herself involved in everything from divorce to money troubles, to physical issues, to car trouble. She yearned for light, witty, water cooler talk and camaraderie in a hallway, any hallway. Aside from her clients, she was alone, in her standard townhouse, with her computer, her cats, and her mess. But thank goodness there was no traffic.

Lena reviewed her calendar. Deadline, deadline, deadline. Release out on Symco, needs pitch. Follow up with social. Pay membership dues, pick up office supplies and notarize proposal. Meeting at 3. Reminder to prep at noon, take shower at 1:30 to be out the door by 2:15. Got it. She scrolled through her emails and deleted eighty percent of them. Between the spam mail, the people she didn't know or care about wanting to connect all day long, the pokes, posts, likes, notices, and the junk snail mail in her business and personal mailboxes, she was inundated with more than enough information. Still, being in the biz, she had to appreciate the effort. Most didn't require feedback from her anyway.

On the computer, she opened and read, deleted, opened and read. One of the emails caught her attention. A well-respected attorney was sending her a new client. What a great way to start the day! Two brothers had developed a new product. They had an idea many thought was brilliant. The medical technology was designed to bridge gaps, reduce costs, and provide benefits on several levels for all stakeholders, consumers, and trade. Lena valued the introduction by someone she respected as a credible source. Though it was coming up on Thanksgiving weekend, she decided to meet with the team as quickly as possible. Hopefully they would be pleased with the extra effort.

4

Still undressed and at her computer, Lena made arrangements to meet her potential new clients and began the preparations for her meeting with Symco. Her sister, Lori, angrily entered the room. She was a couple of years older, dramatic, and intense. She was dressed for work in a professional designer suit, a stark contrast to Lena's sweats. They were opposites in almost every way. She was a "popper," popping in and out of Lena's life with varying degrees and interests, and was rarely around unless something was important to her. She was also a little "off." Lena was sure that her own evolution of patience and indulgence stemmed from their relationship. She felt she maintained a high tolerance for idiosyncrasies and bad behavior, which explained why she was so often surrounded by it. Because of their differences, the two sisters had grown apart over the years. Still, they were family.

"Where the hell have you been?" demanded Lori.

Startled and annoyed, Lena answered, "You know that key is for emergencies. Not that I would ever call you for one."

"Dad says he hasn't seen you."

"He never sees me, even when I'm there. But, it's nice to be missed. I'm working. Never a borrower, never a lender, never late. Still have my first dollar."

Lori quieted and lit a cigarette.

"This is a no smoking zone," said Lena.

Lori ignored her. "If memory serves me, you spent everything else."

"This is true."

At 14, Lena got her first job in babysitting. She found out early on it was easier to make money than to ask her father for it. She set a financial goal to earn $100 in 10 weeks in the days when babysitting paid one dollar an hour and her friends were having fun. She worked the allotted hours, bored and uninspired most of the time.

When she reached her goal, Lena was elated. She spread her single dollar bills all over the bed. She rolled on them like they did in the movies. She threw the dollars up and down, up and down, letting them fall through her fingers. She smelled the money. Each dollar had a distinct "money" smell no matter where it came from.

She wadded the dollars up and stuffed them in her pocket. Then she pulled the wad out of her pocket. Then she put it back in and pulled it out again. "Why yes, I am rich, look at my wad." It was hers, all hers, she exalted, imitating a diabolical laugh. After a week, she promptly spent it save for the lone dollar bill that hung above her computer. And the pattern continued. She liked making money and she liked spending it, but she was never in debt.

"I can't cope, Lena, you know this."

"For once Lori, can you pitch in?"

"It takes me weeks to get over every visit."

"All you have to do is feed him. You don't even have to change him."

"He's not normal."

"You're the barometer? Move along, I have to go."

5

Inside the boardroom sat five middle aged corporate types dressed in variations of black suits. There were three men and two women. Lena wore a red suit and sat opposite the group at the table. Presentation materials stood in front on easels, a PowerPoint slide was projected above on a screen, and marketing packages and materials were laid out on the table.

"Very impressive Lena," said one of the men.

"I especially liked the theme you used for the new Symco prototype. Very clever," said one of the women.

"How would you like to work with us full time?" asked the first man.

Lena was taken aback by the unexpected suggestion. "Oh. Wow. Thank you. I-I would consider the right offer." She was pleased with the idea. It represented a great compliment on her professionalism from a very prestigious global firm.

"Our competitors are pushing regulation and bad publicity to keep us out. We need someone like you to push the cause for people who need the product the most."

"You'd be our right-hand woman. You'll develop strategies and implement them. You'd travel and be present as part of the lead team on everything," said the woman.

"It's a 24/7 job in top management for a multi-billion dollar company. Think about it," said the man as he stood signaling the end of the conversation. "Let us know by the end of next month."

Lena followed his lead and stood up. "Oh, okay. Right. Thank you."

After the meeting, Lena went to visit her father at his condo. The 77-year-old retired physician also lived in a habitat in a cookie-cutter hood, but he had a valet and elevator. She apologized to the valet as she handed him the keys to her 10-year-old beat-up car. She was hoping to appear as if she were "the millionaire next door." She entered the building and took the elevator to the 19th floor. As the elevator doors opened, she was suddenly hit with an unusual mixture of smells. Something along the lines of brisket, grease, baked goods, curry, and cooked peppers made her eyes water and confused her mind. As she approached the designated unit, she heard the evening news blaring through the door.

She knocked on the door. No answer. She banged. No answer. Finally she used her key and let herself in. She walked over to the flat screen, stood in front of it, and waved to the older man on the couch. George Gorman was wearing plaid shorts, white socks with brown sandals, and a colored t-shirt faded with spots. Finally acknowledging her presence, he pressed the remote he held in his hand and pushed the button to shut off the blaring television. Instant silence.

"Hello dear," said George.

"Dad, I've been standing outside the door for ten minutes," said Lena.

"I didn't hear," he said.

"Really?"

"I have a grilled chicken from the grocery store. There's coleslaw and pickles too."

"That's nice."

"Hungry?"

"Five's a little early for me."

"Good, let's eat," he said standing up.

"When was the last time you changed your shirt?"

"Don't need to. It's still good."

"It's okay to wash. You also have 20 more just like it."

"Why waste?"

Lena shook her head in frustration. "Really? No effort for the living?"

Lena walked into the kitchenette with her father in tow. He sat at the dinette while she set the table and pulled out the food. George looked out the window enjoying the view of the Intracoastal. After the table was fully set, he started to eat. Lena sat down to join him.

"By the way, I got a new exciting client today."

"Excitement is overrated. What do you do exactly?" responded her father.

"PR and Marketing. 20 years now." Lena said.

"I don't know what that is."

"No need to."

"While you're up can you get me a drink?"

"I'm not up." She rolled her eyes and sighed. "But I'll get you a drink."

Lena got up and poured soda from the refrigerator.

"While you're up can you put this in the sink?"

George handed Lena his dirty plate and silverware. He folded his used paper napkin carefully and put it back in the napkin holder. "Neatness counts," he said as he got up, exited the room, and shut off the lights while Lena was still in it.

"I'm still here," she said as she sat down to finish.

"We don't own stock in Florida Power and Light."

6

Driving home, Lena reflected on her father. There was no comparison, she decided, between father and daughter. A player in the tail end of the Great Generation, George represented the quintessential first generation born of immigrants. This group appreciated their parents' sacrifices. They knew they must succeed in America no matter what. Growing up during the depression era, her father had always been frugal to the extreme, and by being so achieved the American dream from rags to riches. At 55, he retired with no debt. Home and kids' colleges paid for in full with a nice stash of cash to retire on. He was highly organized, well read, educated, and competent. He was also overbearing and a hard act to follow. His high standards and expectations coupled with his lack of understanding for the next generation often resulted in frustration between himself and his children. However, from time to time they would bond when quoting Ben Franklin in harmony.

Lena tried to be more like her father. She tried to shape her life in his image and gain accolades for making the effort. It was becoming her life's goal.

7

Two days later Lena met her new potential clients at their office. It was sparse with a nice view of the Miami skyline. Two impeccably dressed dark men led Lena to a sitting area in the office. The eldest, Kyle, appeared to be in his late 40s while the younger, Jason, appeared to be in his late 30s. Lena, dressed in a grey suit, sat in the chair while the brothers reclined on the sofa.

"We've heard good things about you. You come highly recommended," said Kyle.

"You as well. I'm eager to learn more about what you're doing and how I can help," said Lena.

"We're involved in medtech. We're working with Fortune 500 companies and running pilots through the University," said Jason.

"I reviewed the website. Very comprehensive and exciting. Looks like you've got it all going on."

"We do. We've been working on this for quite some time. Our mission is to bring affordable and effective healthcare to all," said Kyle.

"When do you expect to launch?"

"In three months. We're going international," said Jason.

They clicked immediately and the conversation continued for another two hours.

"I'd love to be a part of it," said Lena.

"We're counting on that. We're looking for someone who works hard to bring contacts, resources, and marketing skills to the table. Someone with an entrepreneurial spirit like yourself," said Kyle.

"Wonderful," Lena said enthusiastically.

8

Together, Susan and Lena sat in Lena's living room commiserating over wine.

"So, any more thoughts on how you want to spend your time these days?" asked Susan

"Not really. I take direction and build momentum. Not good at the decisions."

"Learn or others will make them for you. Do some personal planning."

"If I take the job with Symco, I'd be giving up my freedom, all of my time, and identity to work 24/7. I'll get paid well but not so exciting. And whatever would be exciting would be overshadowed by exhaustion."

"So, you'd be their bitch?"

"Exactly."

"How's that different from what you're doing now?"

"Well now I'm everyone's bitch."

"Change is good and can lead to other things. Decisions can also be reversed."

"Still, I'd have to give up everything."

They looked around. Susan made a face. "Yeah, eh," she said.

"I did and do everything I am supposed to. And none of it very important."

"What's wrong with that? Important to whom?"

"I want to do something meaningful and interesting."

"Are you really singing the blues? You actually know what the results of the change would be either way. That's the most essential part of any decision."

"That's the problem and yes, the middling blues. I'm a middle aged, middle class, middle of the road kind of gal. I'm unaccomplished, uncommitted, and unfulfilled."

"While we're on the "uns", how about ungrateful?"

"I am grateful. I just want to use my time, energy and passion to bring something meaningful to fruition. I want to focus and commit and see returns."

"What makes you think you're not doing that now? Can't you capitalize on what you already have?"

"It's not the same. I look at my father. Dreams and goals that meant something and were achieved. And everyone benefited. Me, not so much. We have nothing in common."

"I'd say you've had it and got it all. Security, potential, and choices. What more could you want? Different times calls for different...different...." Susan's hands worked the words.

"Measures. What if I can't and don't achieve anything with it?"

"I believe you already have. But, you can keep singing the middling class blues if you want. No one will listen."

"So this is it for me?"

9

Lena saw the vision of the new technology. She was also happy with the team. From the outset, the brothers appeared to have credentials, contacts, and resources to back their project. They consistently name dropped well-known publicly traded companies as partners, some of whom she met, and provided the necessary promotional tools. She was convinced they were going to make it big.

Throwing herself whole heartedly into the project, Lena spent the next few months learning everything she could and then more than she wanted. It soon became apparent that the brothers had founders' syndrome and wouldn't share control or play well with others. The two really believed they were the best in, well everything. Kyle told her, "I have the genes, education, and wherewithal to be the smartest person at the table." Imagine that.

Despite their arrogance, Lena still believed the product and business were sound. And she knew the team was missing three vital elements for success that she could provide: experience, credibility, and resources. She stepped up for the promise of better things to come. She introduced the brothers to reputable companies and exhausted her list of contacts. She created new lists and worked that circle. She found investors and sponsors and worked that angle. She opened new markets and brought in new sales opportunities.

Aside from her work, business, and reputation, Lena loaned her life savings to secure patents and support the business. She was sure they were being honest with her when they said this was a short term bridge loan, she would be repaid in a couple of months, and she would receive lifetime bonuses when the product went to market in just a few months. They had contracts after all.

For the next 15 months, Lena dedicated all her time and effort to the company of two. She dropped her existing clients and sent referrals to colleagues. She worked 16 hour days, 7 days a week, 365 days a year. Everything she had went into their business. She finally had a purpose bigger than herself, with benefits to boot. She was exhilarated and a little tired.

But as time wore on, nagging doubts began appearing like little pop-up windows. Lena was becoming increasingly uncomfortable with the continued push-off of the launch. She was having a hard time explaining why the product was not being launched to the representatives of the international markets she had opened up. Though she had orders for the product, she had no idea where the company was with production, and she seemed to be left out of crucial conversations.

Lena met with the brothers at their office in an effort to find out more about the timelines and expectations.

"The initial campaign is building hype and a base for potential clients and investors. When do you expect distribution to start?" she asked.

"We're holding out for the best offer on distribution," said Jason.

"I thought that was done. Aren't we going to market soon?"

"We'll take care of it. Please continue with the marketing update," said Kyle.

Lena was confused and apprehensive. She hesitated. Until now, she hadn't received any real concrete answers and was growing concerned.

"Okay. We've had great exposure in all the media including a three pager with a lead on the cover of a national trade publication. The social media efforts and analytics continue to bring inquiries, potential customers, positive responses and requests for collaboration."

"Awesome," said Kyle.

"We should begin to review and coordinate the operations and marketing alliances as well as cooperative marketing efforts. Maybe loop in philanthropy. As of now, we have over two dozen markets opened around the world waiting on your delivery. That's the last 15 months in a nutshell."

"We've done a great job. I hope you continue to be part of the team," said Kyle.

"Great, me too. I do have some questions."

"Shoot. We're family," said Jason.

She was uncomfortable and seemed to be reciting from memory. "As you know, I brought investors and potential partners and clients to the table. Yet every time I do that, I'm cut out of the conversation. I believe I should be at the table with the contacts I bring to it. Unless you know of a substantial reason why I shouldn't be there, I'm planning on attending all the meetings I arrange."

"We do appreciate your enthusiasm and didn't want to bother you as your Public Relations expertise is not needed," replied Kyle.

"I wasn't thinking in terms of Public Relations. I was thinking more in terms of the partnership we discussed and the business development work I've been doing all this time for you. I brought these people to the table and part of my compensation is based on making sure the deals happen. How can I do that if I'm not there and involved?"

"I can make the deals happen on my own but you are welcome to attend," said Kyle.

"With that being said, I hope you understand I have a vested interest in this company and the product as well. I do and already did bring experience, credibility, and resources to the mix including all my contacts, new contacts, investors, and sales. I also gave a bridge loan to help secure the patents."

"You're welcome to attend, however, we don't expect you to say anything," said Jason.

Lena was visibly hurt, angry, and more confused. She tried to remain positive.

The next meeting Lena had arranged, she attended it. However, the brothers refused to introduce her. In another meeting someone inquired who she was and Jason replied before she could, "She's just family." From that point forward, she made a point to introduce herself upon entering the room.

When it came to phone conferences she set up, she was told to do the introductions and openings, period. She did as she was told. She also consulted before and after the call on strategy and how to proceed. While on the calls, she consulted via email providing immediate and vital information in addition to key items the brothers inevitably forgot or overlooked during the pitch. She was an integral part of all strategic and tactical plans whether they admitted it or not, and she knew it. She expected and anticipated to be recognized and compensated in the near future.

That's not how it worked out.

At another meeting six weeks later, Lena asked the big question. "When are we launching?"

"Another three months," said Jason.

"Why the delay?"

"We haven't decided who will be our manufacturer," he said.

"The product's not made? Do you have a working prototype? Any designs?" Lena was visibly shocked.

"Oh yeah. We're good. We'll deliver on everything," he said confidently.

"When?"

"Just as soon as we get funding and sign off on all the deals," said Kyle.

Slowly and tentatively Lena said, "I thought you had money for at least the start of development. We're going to want to do that soon, right? We're promoting, selling, and making promises that require us to deliver. I've already taken orders. I'm selling air at this point."

"And people are buying it! Isn't that great?" said Kyle, pleased.

"I don't think so. No." said Lena. This was unbelievable.

10

The next day, Lena sat in her office trying to figure out what she should be working on. Her phone rang. It was Susan.

"Speak," she said.

"How's the launch going?"

"I don't really know. I don't have a clue on what's happening."

"How could you not know?"

"The brothers aren't exactly forthcoming with information. We're total opposites in the way we do business. I don't understand them and just when there's a comfort level, it's gone."

"Clear it up as soon as possible."

"This is so out of my comfort zone. Usually information is clear and things are shared. They not only don't share, they don't really appreciate it when I share. Hard to believe I'm in the communications and people business. I believe in the spin but there has to be a base somewhere."

"You haven't been paid anything for what you've given and invested. Get on the same page. Practice it if you have to. Why are you still with them?"

"They need me. We're doing important work."

"What exactly are you doing?"

Lena was beginning to wonder herself.

Weeks later, Lena had another meeting with the brothers. She still hadn't received any concrete answers from them nor had she been repaid for her loan.

Outside their office door, she practiced what she would say. "You know how much I like working with your company and how I want the product to succeed," she repeated to herself quietly. Taking a deep breath, she finally entered the office, greeted the brothers and sat down.

"I trust all is well and distribution is moving forward. You know how much I like working with your company and how I want the product to succeed."

"Actually, we're in a holding pattern while we wait for the funding to come through for the manufacturing," said Kyle.

Lena's heart sank. She was shaken. She could no longer avoid what was becoming so apparent.

"Still? What happened? You had all those people at the table? There were deals? Do you have any investors or a proof of concept yet? Where are your plans and backing?"

"We're in the process," said Jason.

"Are you saying you don't have one deal executed? I thought you were going to launch over a year ago. I've been fronting my fees and gave you a loan. I'll need to call it in. It was supposed to be repaid five months ago."

"We don't have it," said Kyle.

"Where did it go? You haven't produced anything. Doesn't matter. Please pay me back by the end of the month. I can't afford to give you my retirement fund while I work with no income."

"We'll get it to you when we can," he said.

"You're kidding right? That's not our agreement. I've built hype, publicity, social media, alliances, investment and consumer interest."

"Look, you asked to be a part of all of this and we agreed to it. You haven't really done much and whatever you did hasn't amounted to anything. We don't owe you anything for whatever you think is your time. We did everything pretty much by ourselves," Kyle said.

"We'll pay your loan back when the money comes in," added Jason.

"I'm not an investor. I provided a three-month short-term bridge loan. There's a difference. And yes, I did work for you and you took full advantage of and used everything. In fact, you're still using everything. And despite my best efforts, I haven't even received any real update, financials, or even a request to extend the loan. You haven't given me anything for all that I've done."

"You didn't move one product and your resources are worthless," commented Kyle.

"We don't owe you anything for your time, contacts, and work. We did pretty much everything," repeated the other.

"We'll pay you back your money when we get investors," said Kyle referring to the same people they had lined up for over a year as well as some Lena brought to the table.

"You've had investors and you never produced a product. I presold hundreds of thousands. The orders are pending in two dozen markets. The price can't be finalized because you don't know what it will cost to manufacture. There's no working model. The deals were all on the table but never executed by you. Why? And you're still using my contacts. My God, we really are selling air."

"We'll get back to you if we need anything further," said Kyle.

"What?" Lena exclaimed feeling the blood run from her face.

"This isn't working out," said Kyle.

"So, I give you everything and you give me nothing?"

"We just don't need you anymore," said Jason.

"So I get nothing?"

The reality slowly sank in. Lena felt sick to her stomach. The company had no solid plans or backing. The brothers had no proof of concept, no investors, no funds to pay her back, and no plans for any of it.

11

Work came to an abrupt end for Lena. The brothers cut her out completely but still continued to use her contacts, resources, and work product in their marketing and promotion. Lena tried to reach out to renegotiate her position. They ignored her.

The brothers continued to grow their business, while Lena's was self-destructing. With the help of people they gave no credit to, they seemed to progress and secure meetings with top Fortune 500 companies. Still, they never seemed to get off the ground. There was no launch date in sight. She had a hard time grasping the reality of the situation.

Weeks after her confrontation with the brothers, Lena lay in bed longer than was necessary. She didn't want to move. She had nothing to do, and who cared? Yet, there was a lot to do. She had to rebuild everything. Where does the agenda begin?

After some time, she struggled to pull herself up into a seated position, lifted her eye mask, and peered at herself in the mirror across the room. Her hair was standing up. She looked like a madwoman. "You're so pretty," she said to herself. "It's no wonder you rock the world." She looked up at the locks of hair on her head, slowly pulling and examining them section by section. She began to sob.

She reached over and pulled her laptop off the nightstand. She plopped it in her lap, turned it on and waited for the boot up. She connected to

Google and typed "How to start your career over when you're 50 and broke." She had always been a good typist. All sorts of things came up in the search but nothing that was relevant to her situation.

"I know this is a bad dream. Things will be over soon. If I work hard and keep moving the universe will provide…. AHHH!" she wailed and pounded her fists on the bed, along the sides of her body, of course, so as not to hurt the computer. Arms went up, they went down. They went up, they went down. Who knew for how long?

Slowly, Lena crawled out of bed and began her morning ritual. She had nowhere to go. She moved into the bathroom. She picked up the crab in her sink, looked at her cat, and then threw the crustacean out the window. As she brushed, lather gathered around her mouth. She was foaming. She was a new "American Greed" statistic. She would have to sue and begin anew. That's what people did right? At least that's what she had in mind. Body and actions to follow.

At her computer with tea, Lena started her own Twelve-Step program. She scheduled a meeting with an attorney. Step One. She pulled out her old resume and began to update it. Step Two. This could take a while.

12

Step Three of the new program was to search through job opportunities on the "Grabajob" website. It took hours to review and respond. The online application process was a tedious, ridiculous procedure. She spent 45 minutes on each online application to compete with over 100 people. When she last looked for work, there had been a simple standardized procedure everyone understood. She merely answered classified ads with personal calls and snail mail resumes. There was little up-front time commitment for much more opportunity. It was live. Now she had to sell herself to a computer that used analytics to analyze her and the words she used. It was very stressful.

At 50 and self-employed for two decades, Lena found it hard to find an appropriate job, let alone a pay scale to match. To add insult to injury, the business etiquette of rejections, follow-ups, and letter writing had abruptly left the building. The information age replaced the Age of Aquarius and somehow she had to adjust.

The phone rang just as a popup appeared on her screen that read, "The real estate industry has produced the largest number of self-made millionaires." Lena squinted at the caller id. It was Susan. She could tell because her phone said so.

"Hello." No answer. "Hello. Anyone there? Hello?" said Susan.

"Describe anyone" said Lena very deflated.

"Fat, bald, and happy."

"Strike three."

"Your clients slash imbeciles?"

"AKA Siamese twins attached at the scrotum, yes."

"That's the spirit. What happened? Last I knew you were going to speak with them about being at the bargaining... you know."

"Table. Turns out they didn't want me at the table or in the startup. They only wanted my money, time, resources, and contacts. They left me with nothing. I'm out. After 15 months of giving them everything, I'm out. "

"What about your loan, your other business?"

"I have neither. They took my money and won't give it back. I referred out all my clients and any new ones that came in to an associate. I thought this would be my exit strategy."

"What!?"

"Yep, I drank the Kool-Aid."

"Saw the movie. Everyone dies at the end."

"I got nothing. I was told my time, money, resources and even I are worth nothing, yet they continue to use them all. I really thought this was my exit strategy and I was creating something much bigger than myself. I soooo wanted to do right by the world."

"Yes, I'm sure that was your mission. When I look at you, I think, how generous is she? Did you try to talk to them? Work a deal?"

"I did. They ignored me. I can't even go back to the companies and people I brought to the table because it's so messy. They keep moving forward with my resources and I keep losing ground."

"How do you know? They still may never launch. What happens now?"

"My thought exactly. I don't even know what to do today. And I don't do well in pending."

"Drum up some good business quick like you always do."

"I can't."

"Why not? You sound terrible. I have to run some errands but I'm on my way over."

Susan arrived two hours later. Lena was on the couch, still in her pajamas with her computer sitting on her lap. Her hair had adopted a fondness for standing straight up. She continued to look like a madwoman, possibly worse. The place was a mess shaped by remnants of food, laundry, and general trash.

"CR-A-A-A-P-P!" exclaimed Lena just as Susan walked in.

"What's going on? What's happening here?" Susan asked making a face. "Yikes! You-re, you're all wrong and not so attractive." Susan looked at Lena who has stopped wailing and stared blankly back.

"I'm on the Grabajob website. I've been applying for weeks and haven't received one answer. Last time I applied for a job, we checked the paper, saw an ad. We called live or used snail mail, had an interview and got a yes or no. Now I have to apply online to a computer with the right key words in order to show I'm qualified. It's like a game show."

"Buy a vowel."

"Even with key words, each application takes 45 minutes. So far, I've received one email response for weeks of work. It's for funneling money from Asia. So much for business etiquette. I'm never going to do business with these places ever again. They're mean! Crap, where are my glasses?" Lena felt frantically around her body.

Susan leaned over Lena's shoulder to see what she'd been working on.

"The stem-cell research clinic? Agreed. On your head. Actually, entangled in your hair. Maybe you should you know, journal your thoughts and feelings."

"Why?"

"To ease everyone else's pain."

"I'm throwing it out to the universe! What more can I do? What time is it?"

"You should have taken better care of yourself. Your clock says 3:40."

"That means it's 4:55."

"Isn't it one of those...thingamajigs?"

"Automatic time clock? Why yes, yes it is."

"It's 75 minutes behind?"

"That is correct. It's automatic."

"Huh...." Susan shook her head to clear it.

"I've never not worked or not had work or leads. I feel half of me is missing."

"I'm guessing the better half? Anyway..... Look, you're simply not employee material. Take me for example," Susan looked at Lena. For the first time she noticed how pathetic her friend really looked. She stared at the mess and noticed some kind of spray can.

"What is this?" Susan asked picking up the can from the mess.

"You know...." She mimicked spraying. "Icing."

"What did you do with it?"

"I ate it."

"What?"

"I didn't eat it straight from a can into my mouth. That was last week. I put it on a piece of wheat bread."

"Wow. I, I forgot what I was saying. Oh yeah, I can be an employee, you can't. You're not made that way and simply love the game too much. You function on a different level." Susan put the can of icing out of Lena's reach. "This is the path you chose. It suits you. So, you lost this round. Big deal. At least you're in the game and losing is part of it. But, alas, the game isn't over yet. Utilize your assets and talents. Live the life you chose. That's it, that's all I got. Good luck."

"Interesting, your thoughts. So Aristotle-like. And in full sentences."

"Keep looking for a job. In the meantime, reinvent, do something cool, look cool doing it. You are the most fearless person I know."

"Like what?"

"Look, I did my part. I listened and advised. Don't be so lazy."

"I don't know how to do that."

"You're in marketing. Be creative. Market!"

"I'm the cobbler who has no shoes!" Lena wailed.

Later that week, Lena met with her attorney. He told her she might or might not have a case as there were some loose ends. If she did have a case, the brothers might still never pay her. And everything would take a long time. Litigation would be miserable and costly. On the other hand, if she did nothing, she'd get nothing and would definitely never see her money again. She had to think about it. Maybe she should journal. She'd rather have a shot of tequila.

13

Several more weeks passed, and Lena finally received a somewhat positive response from one of her job applications. There was an opening for a business financial writer. The company created plans and projects as an outsourced firm for Fortune 1000 companies. She received an email informing her that the president wanted to set up a phone interview. She looked at her calendar. There was absolutely nothing on it. She reviewed the attached schedule and chose Thursday at 3:30 from the list of available time slots. Being a professional, she made sure to thank the nondescript email person with her suggestion of the suitable time slot from the list provided.

The next day, just as the email promised, Lena received a call to set up the phone interview. After confirming she had received the email with the available time slots, she again selected Thursday at 3:30. The woman on the other end responded, "Wait. Let me tell you what's available." Lena listened as the woman proceeded to list the same times that were in the email, including Thursday at 3:30. "Thursday at 3:30 is great," said Lena. "Let me check and see if that's available," the woman replied.

By the time the woman confirmed that Thursday at 3:30 was indeed available and they would conference then, Lena had decided she wanted nothing more to do with the company or the job. She would undoubtedly become violent. She had visions of cutting off the woman's head. Clearly she wasn't using it. The violence wouldn't be virtual, but it could indeed go viral.

The following week, Lena had another phone interview with a different recruiter, one who seemed to understand her skills set and experience.

"You're exactly what we need," said the recruiter during the phone interview. "Do you speak any languages?"

"I knew French in college and may be able to resurrect it. I know a little Ebonics and Spanglish as well," replied Lena.

The woman on the other end seemed pleased. She explained the hiring process and what it entailed. Lena was one of 125 applicants. They would be in touch. They never spoke again.

Friends tried to help but "things" happened. Lena was referred by one friend and later hired by another to handle her company's global public relations.

Almost immediately, her efforts created rapid response and high levels of exposure. Then, without warning, her friend cancelled the contract. Despite the cancellation clauses in it, Lena received no explanation or any official notice.

They met in Deborah's office. It was one of the new-age ones with high ceilings showing duct work, wide open spaces, and transparent offices, very exposed and somewhat ugly. Deborah wore sophisticated casual while Lena wore a suit.

"Your work is always so outstanding Lena. You're just the right person to handle the US market. I'd love to give you more work."

"I'm glad you're happy. It's been good for me too."

"We really wanted you to come on board full time."

"Fantastic!"

"The bad news is that the company is in the red despite our best efforts. We have to restructure our marketing. I hate having to do this to my friend of many years."

"What are you doing?"

"I have to let you go, it's not what I want."

"Why would anyone cut their marketing budget when they're in the red? It's the main revenue generating arm of a company."

"Our management is so disorganized."

"Aren't you the COO?"

"Yes, but everything goes through the CEO and the board. They can't decide on anything."

"Don't they typically let you just do what you want?"

"For the most part, yes."

"So how are you going to handle this missing portion? I'd hate to see the momentum we built go away."

"We hired another company to satisfy internal politics. They're much more expensive and deliver nothing. You're truly the best we ever had."

"Can you adjust their contract?"

"We can't. It would get complicated. The language is pretty harsh."

"You can negotiate. You're cancelling mine with no regard whatsoever to my terms."

"What I'd really love is a professional PR retiree who can work for a lot less full time. Any thoughts?"

"Many."

Though it went against her grain, she accepted the news as best she could. What else could she really do? Once again, she was left with no money, no means of support, and no prospects. Time and friends moved on.

14

Lena felt it might be time for some familial support. She was running out of other ideas. She invited her sister and father to dinner. They arranged to dine at George's convenience, 5:30pm, allowing time for the 4:00 stock bell, the financial news commentary of the day, and a little drive time. They met at a casual restaurant, a step above a deli. George and Lena waited for Lori. After five minutes, George gave up and ordered. The waitress took the order and left.

"Bread?" Lena offered her father from the basket.

"Thank you dear," he answered as he took a slice.

"Nothing seems to be working. I don't know what to do."

At that moment, Lori entered with her Gloria Swanson-waiting-for-her-close-up attitude. She swished herself into a seat.

"I'm here and ready to be admired," said Lori.

"Lucky, that's what we are," commented Lena.

"Take the path of least resistance. Don't take unnecessary risks," Dad said to Lena.

"Too late. I thought you liked the road less traveled," answered Lena.

"Yes, that too."

"What day is today?" asked Lori.

"Tuesday," responded Lena.

"I hate Tuesdays."

"We'll have it removed."

"I think I'll become Orthodox."

"You're not finished being a lawyer yet."

"I'll have lots of children to make up for the ones you're not having."

"You could tattoo their names next to the others."

"I'll email you a few ideas. Just remember when emailing back, email and wine don't mix."

"I've noticed."

The waitress started to serve the food.

"Pass the salt dear," said George.

Lena did as she was told. Dinner was over within an hour.

15

Lena sat at her computer giving the job market another chance to recognize her genius. The phone rang. It was Susan.

"Okay, don't get mad," she said before Lena could even say hello.

"I can't commit," replied Lena. "What did you do?"

"I put us on a whatchamacallit site. Where you get hired," Susan said.

"Job site? That's not so bad. Why do you need a job?" asked Lena.

"It's not really a job site. Actually it's a site for freelance gigs. We got one."

"Got one what?"

"Got a gig…for a funeral referral service."

"I'm sorry…. What?"

"Well, it's kind of like party planning, but for a funeral."

"Why, what, how did this come about?"

"I was thinking outside the box."

"Literally?"

"I thought it would be a fun way to make money. We can do it together. Any work is good work right?"

"I beg to differ. I was thinking something a little more, more lively. What is it exactly?"

"There's a funeral in about seven days. The partner of a gay couple died. The bereaved wants us to coordinate the funeral and the reception to follow."

"Well, at least this client can't back out. We'll need a price list with fees, foods, and décor. We'll need photos and the man's life story. We'll need to set all that up and meet ASAP to coordinate venues and a chaplain. Unless he's Jewish. Is he Jewish?"

"I didn't get the impression he was a member of the tribe. No temple listed. I knew you could do it. John Wilton Marsh."

"Everything I do, I've never done before and yes, money is money I suppose. I'm online checking this guy out. This guy was loaded. What did he do?"

"Yes, it's something. Real Estate."

"Ah, okay, one less realtor. I'm sorry. I'm so distracted and negative with the lawsuit. The brothers are arguing everything. They are actually now fighting the collateral for the loan."

"You knew they were going to dig their heels in. I would do the same I suppose."

"Why can't we just make a deal?"

"If you guys could, you wouldn't be in this situation."

"Yes, but why do they always have all the control over everything? I have no control even over my own life."

"Because everybody gives it to them. Cheer up; we have a funeral to attend."

Lena and Susan met their new client at his house. The plentiful peacocks were beautiful but made lots of freaky noises, like crying babies. She thought the house was quaint in an old Florida style with lots of foliage. The grieving partner provided details and insight into family dynamics. He outlined what he wanted and needed to happen. Lena took the framed photo of the deceased.

She stopped by the print shop to have the photo enlarged into a laminated poster. When she took the photo out of the frame, she noticed there was another photo behind it. It was from a race car driver expressing his affection for the deceased. "Oh my," she said. Lena called Susan.

"I have a photo of another person behind the photo of the deceased. There's a note on it. It's a love note."

"Don't say anything."

"What if it's a star in the race car industry and the photo is worth something?"

"Leave it be Lena."

"I have to know the story."

"Don't you have enough on your plate? Leave innocent people alone."

"Why?"

Susan hung up and Lena went home. The week of activity passed and it was now game time at the church. The poster was placed on a stand in the front near the flowers. Digital photos rotated above in a montage on a screen. Music played softly in the background. The family arrived. It was everything the bereaved hoped it would be. Susan and Lena stayed awhile to make sure all was okay.

Lena found funerals the best part of a sad situation. Some were filled with jokes and lively discussion. Some were filled with idiots who didn't know what to say but liked the limelight so they shared anyway. All personalities were exposed.

Lena noticed the tension immediately between the family and the lover. One relative brought his own cameraman to preserve his mourning for all eternity. He knelt at the casket with tears in his eyes. He directed the cameraman to shoot the best angle of him crying. They didn't want to miss anything. Perhaps he would post it on YouTube, Facebook, LinkedIn, and Pinterest or use it in a portfolio. It was too good not to share.

Lena and Susan left the action to set up the reception at the house. The two prepared all the fixings aside from the main dish, which the family insisted on having delivered. While they waited, they arranged the appetizers, drinks, side dishes, and desserts, feeling very pleased with themselves and the elaborate display they had organized.

When the family arrived, members rearranged all of it. Susan was not happy.

"Look at those cankles." she said. "Aren't those the ugliest feet?"

"What are cankles? I can't keep up," commented Lena.

Finally, the funeral party was over. There were lots of leftovers that neither wanted. Lena kept the crackers. Susan took the meatballs. They each made $1000. Only 99 more to go.

16

Rebuilding her life would take energy and ambition. Lena wasn't sure she had enough of either left. But there was no choice. She had to plow forward. She knew there would continue to be many challenges. Everything was so different now. In the roaring 80s, she was filled with dreams, vitality, and inspiration. At 50, in a whole other millennium, she didn't want to rebuild, didn't plan for it, hadn't had to, and was angry she had to do it now. She was not interested, enthusiastic, energized, or inspired. She was bitter, bitter, bitter.

To begin, she had to connect. She had to connect with people, with Facebook, with LinkedIn, with Instagram, with everything out there. And once connected, she had to connect some more with pokes, likes, and 500 plus connections. And once connected, she had to be responsive, immediately. She was burnt out just from the connections.

Lena also didn't take well to unemployment. She was beginning to lose her mind after weeks of isolation with nothing to do except face repeated rejections. She began to notice all the broken things in her house and grew anxious about fixing them. The place was getting messier and out of control. The more she stayed home, the more things she had out of place and the more dishes she had to wash. She had no idea how they multiplied. She only had one mouth.

Her cats became a focal point for her. They were homeless when she took them in. She never named them, so she called them "Thing 1" and "Thing 2."

She studied and observed them at great length. She began to follow their patterns. They often got in the way. She stepped over them as they slept quietly on their backs or around them when they tried to play tag with her. Other times they walked on her or ran across her computer, ruining whatever document or application she was working on at the time. They seemed to be annoyed by her work and in retaliation ate her papers.

If she was watching television or sleeping, one or the other would fly out of nowhere and pounce on her chest. They cried in the background and snored in the foreground. They had hairballs. To thank her for her hospitality they brought her gifts - birds, rats, squirrels, crabs, frogs, garden snakes, and a multitude of lizards. She moved them off her keyboard, chair, and papers. Sometimes they sat on her head or the back of her chair with a tail swatting her face. Today she removed one curled up in her sink so she could brush her teeth. He screeched. The other sauntered out from a pile of clothes wrapped in a once-white grey bra.

17

As her humiliation and frustration grew, Lena felt she was losing her grasp on life. She was becoming outdated and irrelevant. After months of discouraging attempts to get a job, it was time to take charge again. She finally committed to doing something on her own. Step Four. Out of desperation she came to the conclusion that real estate might be a possible solution. It was the only thing she could think of at the moment where age and status made no difference.

Though the investment side was where she really wanted to be, Lena didn't have the money. Her instincts were also not as sharp as they should be and her confidence was surely shot to hell. She took motivational classes and investment seminars that she thought might help.

Her efforts were less than encouraging. It was hard to sit still, do the math, and stay focused. Her fidgeting was disruptive to others. The woman next to her let her know it with very loud body language.

The instructor pontificated: "I originally started out as a real estate agent. It lasted a day. I drove a friend to see two houses. I told my client friend, 'Here are two houses. They are exactly alike in the same subdivision. Pick one.' He did and that was the last time I ever showed property as a realtor. The service industry was never for me. I'm in the money industry. You can be too."

Lena had questions. "Can you go over the math again? I'm just not getting it."

"The money industry isn't for everyone," he replied.

18

Undeterred, Lena listened to and continuously repeated money affirmations to open up the universe and build confidence. She repeated, "Money comes easily and effortlessly to me. I am a money magnet. Opportunity is boundless. I deserve, appreciate, and cherish money. Please give me some." She shared goodwill and extra happiness wherever she went, hoping for good karma to kick in. She greeted herself every morning with "Good morning Sunshine" and cheered herself on throughout the day. "Oh beautiful, wise, competent, rich one, how shall we create the money flow today?" Some questioned her sanity as she passed them by.

Lena knew exercise was as important as the mental training to keep her relaxed, focused, and in the zone. It was also helpful in case she ever found herself in a hospital and needed to be confident and firm when she flashed her backside for all the world to see. Step Five.

Donned in her old leg warmers, she headed to the gym to get pumped, finally using the lifetime membership she had bought years ago. Driving through traffic she played her 80s hits CD to get in the mood. She danced in the car to "YMCA" by the Village People, looking a bit like an epileptic with Tourette's syndrome. She had recently upgraded her exercise routine to the "Train to Win" class. Thirty seconds hard on the spin cycle, 30 seconds harder, 30 seconds recovery, followed by a headstand with push-ups as the big finish. She was the most animated participant in the class, until she collapsed onto the floor. "I'm 50," she exhaled, her arms and legs limp and rubbery. "I'm in the zone...." Why exactly did people pay for this?

Two women next to her spoke amongst themselves. They agreed that "gym" rats will die of heart attacks. They were going to take it easy just to be safe.

Susan met up with Lena in the parking lot on the way out. "Working it all out huh? Good times to come. New career, new way of doing things. Same old workout clothes."

"If it weren't for the fact that they took my life's savings and my livelihood, I wouldn't mind. I can't even get a job at my age, especially after being on my own for so long."

"Why real estate?"

"They'll take anyone."

"Why not go back to your business?"

"I can't."

"Just stay the course, whatever you do. Figure out how long you're gonna live and work backwards from there."

"I'm a statistic with not too many choices. No one's interested in talent and experience, only cheap or overpriced and unproductive labor with key words. But I'm pumped, excited, and believe in the universe. And now I'm selling the American Dream."

"Stay focused, something will pop. You could be a statistic the other way too - rags to riches. You always do fine when you focus. Let the... guys... you know...."

"Lawyers. I can't focus."

"Yeah, those guys. Let them take care of the rest. Try Sudafed. Take two, helps with middle age."

"I took Fish Oil. I need money; I'm flat broke. This isn't what I planned. I was supposed to be rich. I followed all the rules."

"But in someone else's game where there are none. You're just on a new journey, could be a better one. Certainly interesting. Exactly like you wanted. "

"Yeah, no. Not really interested."

"Did you speak to your psychic?"

"Yeah. I think she was in the middle of seizure."

The next day, it was Zumba. Oh boy! The Italian-Argentine female instructor was fashionably late. During the class, she snapped her fingers dramatically to alert all of a step change. One wouldn't have known otherwise. Lena danced to her own beat and added a few more steps in her head. She picked up the pace when 70s and 80s music played. The instructor told her she prayed for her. Lena thought this was so thoughtful.

Maybe a 6 a.m. cardio cut class would work. The group of 65-plus year-olds was punctual and perky. The instructor introduced everyone. She wondered if Lena would be able to keep up. "These people have been doing this for years," she said. Lena was confident. She worked out from time to time. However, she had never worked out to Classic Rock before, especially at this hour. She found the music and their lyrics both distracting and disturbing for an early morning workout. She relished watching the others move and groove to "Live and Let Die" and "Spirit in the Sky". She barely could keep up in her zone. The female instructor made lewd comments to her and Lena could swear she was being hit on.

Next, she gave the strength-training class a shot. She lifted weights to her head, lowered them to her shoulders, knees, and toes, raised them back to her knees, and lowered them to her toes. One definitely had to have some kind of rhythm in these classes. Lena seemed to have misplaced hers. Her mind wandered. She lost count. Then she lost control of her gliders. They flew across the room. She was rattled. Her next exercise depended upon these gliders.

It was a tough class. These new exercises were unnatural and illogical. Lena missed basic aerobics, jazzercise, Richard Simmons, and Jane Fonda. She cheated and did one move for every two counted. The instructor was watching and reminded her that the class was for her benefit. Lena was okay with it; she knew she could buy a Brazilian butt.

Lena tried yoga next and found she was pretty good at it. She decided yoga was the best class for her and all those 50 and above. The clothes were more civilized and elegant. And she wouldn't have a heart attack like the gym rats. She wasn't crazy about the music though. The gym was definitely musically challenged. The 70s Muzak collection featured old songs about tragic love and life losses. It was a bit of a downer.

As Lena hummed the theme to "Brian's Song," she focused her mind, body, and soul away from her constant visions of violence directed at anyone that annoyed her. This included the woman to her right, who was slowly invading her personal space. The woman to her left moaned in ecstasy with almost every pose. "Focus on the breathing" Lena admonished herself. "So you don't pass out." She figured overall it might be best if she followed lefty's lead and moaned in unison.

She moved into her poses with intense concentration. Her tongue slowly slid over her top lip. She scrunched her face in deep deliberation. Sweat rolled down her brow. She was doing well. She was working the "pose of the dancer" and held her right foot behind her in her right hand like a bow. The left hand faced straight out in front of her. She tilted first to the floor and looked down. As her gaze moved up, her body followed and tilted upward. She looked further and further ahead on the floor in front of her with each slight rising tilt. As she did this, she saw another classmate's foot. When she tilted up even further, her gaze continued to travel up his leg. The leg was perfect. It was absolutely perfect. She kept tilting and gazing, tilting and gazing, up to the top of his leg. Then she fell flat on the floor. The instructor inquired if she was okay. "I'm good, I got it, no worries," Lena mumbled as she tried to regain her balance in mind, body, and soul, as well as her composure. When the session was finished, she quickly packed up her things and left. She jumped into her car, which was parked on a strange angle across two spots, turned on her music, and drove away to James Brown. "Aww, I fee-ee-l good! Like I knew I would...." Yep, yoga was the one for her alright.

19

Lena mustered up enough positive energy and enthusiasm to learn more about business in general and real estate in particular. "Well, this is my last shot," she said to herself as she stared at her new real estate license, cards, and a map of south Florida. She wanted to be savvy. She wasn't sure what would happen, but she kept busy meeting hard working, motivated people and studying the material. She worked diligently to make an effort to move forward, be productive, and stay positive. It was an uphill battle.

First she had to start with the basics. What brokerage firm or agency should she go with? There were hundreds. Lena didn't want her own brokerage office with overhead and liability. She knew her limits and didn't want to care for others. The first broker she signed with was none too helpful, despite the fact that she stood to receive a large percentage of Lena's commissions. Lena changed agencies to one in Miami for a better deal. No matter which broker's office she signed with, she still had up-front costs that never seemed to end.

Lena was accustomed to carrying her own business expenses as well as being the backend, frontend, support, and delivery on everything. She was well informed about the tax advantages, pitfalls, expenses, budgets, and maintaining supplies. She just wasn't prepared for or interested in starting a brand new business. Bitter, bitter, bitter. The new broker made the transition easier by providing substantial office support and live people available to assist her at no extra cost. This was an essential element to building her real estate empire. Everything, including her, was in place and ready to go.

She liked her office. It had a water cooler. Computers and a conference room were available any time. Paperwork was processed by the staff. She felt safe and secure. Her broker kept the office upbeat with humorous memos and emails. Just that morning she received an email providing stats on why sex is good for sales. She shared it with friends.

The associates in the office were mostly Hispanic. Not knowing a word of the language, Lena often smiled and nodded. They liked her because she was the most agreeable person in the office. She felt special. They fed her, the token gringo, all kinds of interesting dishes, and communicated with her in Spanglish sign language. Lena found this helpful as she was beginning to forget most words anyway.

"Hola, coma esta bien et tu?" she'd say.

"Okay, okay. Café?" replied the office manager.

"Gracias," replied Lena.

The woman continued to speak to her in Spanish. Lena didn't understand but smiled and nodded anyway. The woman laughed, hugged her, and offered her more food. Lena examined it and accepted. She proceeded to a computer where she intended to spend the rest of the day.

At the computer station, Lena hammered away in deep absorption. Suddenly, there was a "Bamm!" She jumped off her seat and barely landed back down on it. Steading herself, she looked up. Her broker was standing over her smiling.

"You responded very well," he said.

Lena was stunned. Finally able to recover her speech she spilled out, "T-Thanks. To what? Why? W-What happened?"

"I hit the back of your seat really hard. It works better if you lean forward more. Most people lean forward to look at the computer but you were too far back to do the slam really loud. You should hear the noise when I have more space. It's really, really loud!"

"I see." Lena nodded dumbfounded, not seeing at all.

"I do the slam with Lourdes all the time. You should see her. She screams and screams, pauses, looks you straight in the face, and then keeps screaming. She doesn't stop. It was so bad one day that the people downstairs wondered if someone was being attacked. It was great!"

Lena was surprised, curious, horrified, confused, and amused. Her face wore all the emotions. "Please make sure to do it sometime when I'm here so I can enjoy it as well. Then we'll record it, add video and put it on YouTube. Why waste a bloodcurdling scream?"

"Fantastic idea! I love it, love it…," the broker trailed off as he left the room. Her phone rang and she picked it up expectantly. Time to start selling something!

"Hi Lena," said her attorney.

"Crap," replied Lena.

"Why crap? I haven't said anything yet."

"You will."

"Could be good news."

"When is speaking with an attorney ever good news? Everywhere I turn I'm surrounded by them and it's never good. Have you met my sister?"

"The other side wants to settle."

"Money?"

"No."

"Oh, so, air?"

"The original loan, interest, fees, money, and stock. If they default, you get an automatic judgment and extra."

"Everything I was entitled to a year ago. How nice. So they want to give me what I already am supposed to get and in return I give them more time?"

"Correct."

"Are they on the market?"

"No. But they say any day now."

"Why should I settle?"

"How much do you believe? A trial can go either way, always."

"I just don't get how they can demand this kind of deal when I'm holding all the cards."

"Yes, you do have control. The deal is up to you."

"Really? It doesn't feel that way. Okay, what's three more months? Do it."

"Done."

Lena hung up and commented to herself, "Oh lovely one, beautiful lady, you'll do well after all. I deserve, appreciate and am grateful for all that I have - despite the fact that I had more and the rodents took it."

20

Continuing her investment classes, Lena learned more about real estate, stock options, tax certificates and deeds, and other investments. She was becoming an enlightened sophomore. She teamed up with a classmate, John, his daughter, and his associate Gail. They were ready to test their investment wings. It was all so thrilling. It was the first time in a long while that she felt so positive.

As it turned out, John had some professional turmoil in his life as well. He was an attorney working on a class action lawsuit against a heavy hitter. He made a deal with the defendant. He would settle the case for his clients to their advantage, but only under the condition that he switched sides. This way the defendant could stop him from bringing any further lawsuits against the company. He had to choose between making the deal, being disbarred and losing his livelihood or spending 10 more years fighting for the livelihoods of others with no guarantees of any outcome which would cost him and his clients dearly.

He made the only choice he felt he could. He signed the deal for his clients, immediately putting himself out of business. John's clients received their monies as agreed. They repaid the favor by hiring fast talking, unethical ambulance chasers who then sued the now disbarred attorney for malpractice. His clients lost everything to the new lawyers. It was a true lose-lose. The land of the free and the brave did not always provide monetary justice for all thought Lena. Bitter, bitter, bitter.

Though he desperately missed practicing law, John told Lena if he was given the choice again, he would do the same thing because he felt it was the right thing to do. Now he was in real estate. They both agreed they had paid their dues and it was time to get it all back.

Together, Lena and the team researched and visited interesting sites, mostly slums. Always it seemed there was a toothless manager. John couldn't bring himself to move forward on slums. It simply was too much for him. Unfortunately, it was the most lucrative and quickest way to make money in real estate. They were facing their first serious dilemma.

Lena and Gail agreed to a more palatable strategy for John. The two women would go big with slums while John stayed in the background. This strategy and the projected numbers helped him overcome his feelings of guilt.

They also agreed they would not limit themselves to South Florida. After an extensive search, the team found a transient hotel in Indiana that intrigued them. The property had over 100 units or "doors" as the lingo dictated. They arranged a visit. Upon first blush, it was a mess, the kind someone could make a killing on if the deal worked out.

Everyone was rather pleasant. The owner arranged for the trio to be shown everything. The gay manager and his partner took great pains to present details, including their own ideas on how to the place could generate more money. They reviewed financials, incentives, and return on investment. Lena was impressed with the knowhow. She was even more impressed with how they had renovated and decorated their own complimentary unit, or two.

It had been a long day, and the weariness was taking its toll. The threesome thanked the couple for their time and effort and departed to their rooms. They were pleasantly surprised that management supplied their bathrooms with Dove soap and Crest toothpaste. Thoughtful.

But the rooms themselves were consistent with their first impression of the rest of the property. Lena pretended they were elsewhere. She was just too tired to care. They had a lot of work to do the next day and she needed her sleep. Without the required seven or eight hours, she was crazy. She was an active growing gal after all.

It was cold. From her valise, Lena pulled out and put on her long johns and sweater. She studied the pillow and contemplated putting her head on it. Pulling out an extra shirt, she wrapped it securely around every inch of the pillow. She stretched out on the bed and just as she was about to fall asleep, she heard loud noises outside her room. Evidently this end of the building was the hang-out area for tenants of this fine establishment.

Then her phone rang. Gail had found a bed bug. Lena, having never seen one before, was curious and a little thrilled. What an adventure! She called John and told him the good news. They all met in Gail's room. There it was, right on Gail's bed. Gail took a photo on her cell phone. They looked it up on Google to be sure. Yep, it was a bed bug alright. She was never going to be able to sleep. John looked Lena up and down in her long johns. "Pack up Phyllis Diller," he said.

They snuck out, hiding in the shadows. They didn't want to insult the staff who had shared so much of their time, the Dove soap, and Crest toothpaste. They crept along the dark parking lot, passing their car, and entered the chain hotel next door. Lena and pals checked in, and within minutes they fell into nice, clean beds. All slept soundly.

The next morning, the little group ravaged the free breakfast buffet. They poured extras into their pockets and bags for later. They were ready and set for the day. They snuck back to the slum, arriving seconds before anyone could discover their absence. Together, Lena and her posse toured the property. They saw most of the rooms, good, bad, and ugly. Most of them were ugly. The roof needed to be fixed - actually, replaced. The stairs were dangerous. It was a perfect investment.

The worker bee tenants told the team there was no budget to do the appropriate work. The toothless souls said they often took funds out of their own pocket for such necessities as nails. Lena and her friends were disgusted. They shared their Dove soap and Crest toothpaste with those who had remaining teeth. Lena's world seemed so far away.

The team then studied the rent rolls as they had been taught to do in class. They confirmed the long-standing contract with the Department of Corrections. Once released, this was often the first place the inmates stayed as they made their way to a new life. The camaraderie and family feeling the tenants had for the place and for each other were obvious.

All of this prompted the threesome to put in an offer. However, the asking and offer prices were too far apart. The current owner wouldn't negotiate down despite all the work that needed to be done. Disappointed, the team left the charm of the big city and ugly hotel for sunny South Florida. Undaunted, they continued their search for the perfect property to create steady passive income.

They put offers on everything. They even came close to actually owning a property. However, as the closing date approached, John backed out. He wanted to "flip" the contract before closing. He thought that holding onto a property without income was risk. Lena thought the property was a real gem. She believed it could be sold later in the year for a substantial profit. Nevertheless, John was the one with the investors and their money, and he did not want to buy and hold the property. She was the poor follower. Being a follower meant she had to go against her gut sometimes. After several months, they ended up with nothing except the knowledge that they traveled well together and enjoyed each other's company.

21

But Lena didn't give up. She knew there was opportunity to be had. She approached a friend in the community who she respected and trusted. He was a contractor with vision. He had software that handled math. She felt empowered. They found a property they liked. It was an old convenience store they intended to redevelop for class A tenants. They ran numbers and promptly overpaid for it. Lena really wanted something with income attached. As a follower, though, she had to be open to ideas.

She invested what little money she had left into the small commercial building and prayed. They had two signed letters of intent before they even closed. They also managed to acquire a grant from the city for renovations. Wow! Things couldn't have been any easier. But then her partner refused to close before leases were signed. Tenants wouldn't sign a lease until the new owners actually owned the building. Eventually, both tenants got tired of waiting and bowed out.

Lena and her partner had to find new tenants. It was a tough sell when only plans were presented. In addition, Lena and her partner couldn't renovate because they didn't know if they had one tenant or two. She wished she had a property with existing cash flow attached. She wondered how and if they were going to come out ahead. Passive income came with a lot of effort.

22

Feeling low but determined, Lena went about her daily chores. Cleaning was not high on the list but grocery shopping was. She had to eat. Since she hated shopping, she did it early in the morning to get it over and done. If she went early enough, she would avoid as many people as possible and zip through the lines, in and out. As she entered the store, despite the fact that there were very few people there, a woman still managed to run into her, even with a wheelchair.

Once inside, she went to the lottery counter and turned in the ticket she hoped was a winner. Her father always thought gambling was the sign of the devil. Still, she played the game, though she had no clue how it worked. The computer spit out the ticket with "Not a Winner" stamped on it in big bold letters. Bitter, bitter, bitter.

Next she visited the pet food aisle. She went to the appropriate locale and stared at the assortment of cans. A man stood next to her, also staring. "You got to get 'em what they want or they won't eat it," he said. She knew he was right. She had to pick and choose carefully for the Things.

Then she went over to the produce section. She stood in front of the apples. There were so many choices. She remembered when the choice was a simple one, green or red. She stared at the names - Jonathan, McIntosh, Red Delicious, Fuji, Cortland, and Pink Layyy-Deeesss. She studied the display in deep silence until...

"Sa-a-adie!! Sa-a-adie!" a woman with a thick New York accent yelled. Lena jumped.

Sadie apparently didn't answer. So, again the woman bellowed.

"Sa-a-adie!!! Sa-a-adie!"

This made Lena unhappy. Sadie finally responded.

"What?" Just as loud and whiney.

"Is three ninety-nine good for fresh strawberries?"

"I have strawberries."

"I didn't see strawberries."

"They're frozen. They're in the freezer."

"Well you didn't tell me that. Are they just as good?"

"Why wouldn't they be good?"

This continued. Lena's ears hurt. She practically ran to the checkout counter. But not before she picked up toilet paper and noticed for the first time how astronomically expensive it had become. She might have to limit her use.

At the checkout counter, the cashier moved rather slowly. She was preoccupied with checking her phone for texts and reviewing Lena's items. It didn't appear she knew she was supposed to be customer service oriented. She commented on almost everything Lena was buying. Her slowness and attitude defeated the whole purpose of shopping early in the morning. Lena packed up her own groceries in thin plastic bags, collected her extremely long receipt, and left in annoyance.

Lena stopped by the "Only for a Dollar" store on her way home where she hoped to buy a much needed dishwashing wand. Naturally, she bought two dollars more than she intended, but it was okay because everything was so cheap. Of course, the items she bought were items of necessity, including the incense to clear her head.

At home in peace and quiet, Lena placed the groceries on the counter and the wand on the sink. She lit the incense and opened the cupboards to replace "bad" food with "good." She would eat only power food from now on.

"No more gluten, dairy, sugar. Add sweet potato, spinach, health bars. Oh, yummy, that looks good."

Lena unwrapped a health bar and put it on a napkin. The phone rang.

"Hello, this is Lena."

"Is Lena there?"

She hung up. "What I did I just say?" she asked the phone.

23

As she dressed for the office, Lena said her affirmations. "I cherish and deserve all that the universe wants for me. I am grateful for all the abundance I have. Money comes easily and effortlessly to me...." She put on her floating heart necklace.

After she finished putting herself in some semblance of working order, she exited her abode and aimed for the car. The twigs on the ground reminded her of lunch. She picked up a few and held them to the sky.

Mimicking Scarlett O'Hara in *Gone with the Wind*, Lena cried out, "As God is my witness, I'll never go hungry again!" She got in the car with her health bar and twig.

While she drove, she sang and danced wildly to her 80s tunes. She shimmied. Other cars kept their distance. She pulled up to a stop light and waited. She looked over at the driver on her left and nodded. The driver and passengers nodded back. It was a road thing.

"Yeah, that's right. I'm cool."

On her right she saw a building with a sign that said, "Alternative Life." She wondered what the alternative was.

From the seat next to her, she picked up the health bar now melted into the napkin. She was hungry and ate it anyway. The people in the other car look disgusted. "What? I'm hungry!"

24

Lena continued her lawsuit while building a new career and vision for herself. The process was disturbing and exhausting. The defendants dragged her through the courts over every little thing. Still, she hung on. She was winning the suit, losing all her money, and gaining debt. The lawsuit, giving up her firm, and the idea of starting over weighed heavily and pained her. Nothing would ever be the same again. She struggled to stay focused on other things.

Shortly after changing agents and getting settled in her new career, Lena had landed two deals, a commercial sale and a lease. This was a great start. However, four months later she found herself with no new closed deals, mounting credit card debt, and for the first time in her life, bad credit. She did the credit card dance and got discombobulated. Finally, she was cut off. She managed to pick up a little marketing work and barely made it through the year.

Lena was stressed and not getting much sleep. She kept replaying the past over and over in her mind. She would calculate and recalculate credit card balances and bills doing unfamiliar math equations in her head. She couldn't concentrate or relax. She watched late-night television until the wee hours of the morning and soon became enlightened in ways she never expected. She watched as a whole family was healed by an evangelist. He healed the people from a disease that was going to attack their house that very same weekend! They were saved because he healed them in advance and stopped the disease from coming! A proactive healer. If only she knew one.

The commercial breaks were hopeful as well. One showed a big church outing at the casino. Another promoted the healing of the debt on Good Friday. The commercial demonstrated people bringing their bills and papers to the church to be healed. All the bills and debts would be healed if people would just bring them to the chapel on Good Friday - and donate. She added that to her to-do list and recorded the appointment on her phone. "Heal debt on Good Friday." She wondered if it mattered that she was Jewish and broke.

She needed sleep. One of Susan's friends sent her some pills to "take the edge off." The friend was dying of cancer, yet she felt that Lena needed the meds more than she did. It took Lena some time to figure out the pills were Xanax, though the dosage wasn't clear. Lena was moved by the fact that a very sick person she didn't even know was sharing the only thing she could - and a valuable commodity at that. It was *that* important. Lena had become dependent upon the kindness of strangers.

A doctor's daughter as well as a former active advocate in anti-drug addiction forums, Lena knew better than anyone the dangers of taking someone else's drugs and meds without a prescription. Even so, she gave into temptation out of desperation and exhaustion. She split one pill into four segments and took a quarter of the pill. She was out the moment she returned to bed. She slept until her normal waking time and remained in a fog the whole next day. She had a very calming feeling. Unproductive, but calming. No Zumba or exercise today.

The dose of serenity actually worked out quite well. Sluggishly, she attended a meeting with her attorney and the brothers to discuss the never ending settlement. A mediator was also present. Lena was smooth. The brothers opened up the negotiation by saying she was nothing and was attaching herself to a rising star. She sat, eerily calm. She didn't even try to hit them. It threw everyone completely off. The negotiation was over before it started.

Returning to her home office, Lena strutted to the kitchen smiling a goofy smile and set the water for tea. She steeped the teabag and fried her oatmeal. Remembering the old anti-drug commercial, she said cheerfully to the empty room, "This is my brain; this is my brain on drugs."

25

After months of no income or prospects and feeling lost, Lena finally consulted with her broker.

"What do I do?" She whined.

"Work harder and smarter. Everyone buys Florida at some point. Market as many properties as you can. Sign up for referral services. Grab any "for sale by owner" property you see. Ask friends for leads. Build your database. Do everything. Go to every networking program possible," he said.

"Hmm." Lena said slowly in deep contemplation.

"Well, what are you waiting for? If you want the dime, you have to put in the time"

"Yes, well, okay then. I just... I don't like pressed chicken. By the way, why aren't the listing agent and selling agent the same thing?"

"Really? Really? I don't know. They just are."

Lena left and walked back to her cubicle and computer desk. In Spanish sign language her office mate who sat next to her asked her why a nice, educated, upper middle class American Jewish woman couldn't make deals. "Jewish yes, chosen, no," Lena explained with arms flying. She still needed to figure out why the listing agent and the selling agent weren't one in the same. She realized she knew very little and needed to become an expert on everything and quickly.

The phone rang. She put the caller on speaker.

"Hello, this is Lena."

"Hi Lena. My name is Tom. I'm looking for a three/three oceanfront property with a direct ocean view."

"Great, what's your budget?"

"Two hundred. How soon can you get it?"

Lena hung up.

Her broker who suddenly was standing behind her and listening asked, "Why did you hang up on that guy?"

"Prank call."

26

Lena knew she needed to hustle and network live to develop the local personal relationships that were necessary for success in real estate. Step Six. Anyone and everyone could use or refer a real estate agent. It was going to be tough. Though she had always been in the people business, she was skeptical of most people and hesitant to meet more. On top of that, she had her fill of compressed foods and fried appetizers.

It hadn't always been like this. During the time Lena had her PR business, she attended business functions regularly. She enjoyed the social aspect of her work and made valuable connections. Back then the networking was great for visibility for both her clients and herself. Back then she could walk on high heels comfortably and not pay for it afterwards. Back then she smiled and meant it. She was in a better place, back then. Everyone, including her, was moving forward back then. This time it was to be all about her. She would only market to get clients, not for clients. She would have photo ops, visibility, and new contacts for sales and referrals. This was new and would be difficult. She had no idea how to pitch herself in this new business. She did her best to get excited. She set up an intense schedule of networking functions for inspiration, support and leads. Yippee! And... bitter, bitter, bitter.

Susan called. "Did you talk to your broker?"

"He said I'm supposed to network and hit up my friends."

"So network. I'm not in the market."

"The thought of getting out and networking again makes me ill. I did it for 20 years and never thought I would ever have to do it again. What do I even say about myself? I'm so angry and tired. And who can wear those shoes?

"Shakespeare, right?"

"I have to get a new photo. I have to be seen live. People are going to know what I look like. Crap."

"You say crap a lot."

"It fits."

27

Alas, it was time for Lena to finally cut and dye the grey out of her hair. She was beginning to look like she had a mop on top of her head.

"It's been so long, how could you let it go? You have grey all over and hair gone wild!" exclaimed her hairdresser Andy. "What's up with you?"

"I know, I know. I think I should shave my legs too though I wear pantyhose and pant suits most of the time. With my eyesight changing I'm not sure what kind of growth I have there but it's been six months so maybe it's time."

"A wax would be nice."

"I try to paint my nails too but I can't sit still long enough for them to dry and end up smudging. Then I don't know what happened to the smudge. I mean where did the smudge go? What's going on with you? You're a little off."

"Happy pills baby, relieves the pain from my hip surgery."

"That's good. Seems to be all the rage. At least it's done," she said, thinking that was the end of it. But, alas, no!

"Yes, I was homebound for a couple of days. You know they take the femur and scrape this and then they take the other bone and scape that and then they do this to the hip and that and.... "

Lena tried three times to end the conversation. Not only was she not interested, but if Andy kept talking about the intricacies, she thought she might vomit. Taking the femur conversation out in public was one dangerous game.

Finally, the cut and dye was over. She was surprised it came out as well as it did. Apparently, the limping and nonsensical slurred speech patterns didn't slow the guy down or alter his perspective.

In her robe after her shower and shave, Lena vacuumed the lint off her clothes. She recited her affirmations as she did so. "Prosperity is my birthright. I have and deserve abundant living. I live a life of passion and purpose." She finished with the vacuum cleaner and pushed the button for the retractable plug. It smacked her in the face.

She dressed sharply, argued with her pantyhose, and added the appropriate accessories. She wanted to be perfectly coiffed all around. Her cats observed her every move with contempt.

Well-groomed and hoping to appear well-heeled, Lena drove up to the sponsoring venue for her first networking event in years. It was a high-flying place with a chandelier in the carport. As had become the norm with valets, she handed over the keys and apologized. She stepped out of the vehicle. Crumbs from her last meal fell across the red carpet as she entered the fine establishment.

Working the glamorous room, Lena remembered the old days. She greeted a familiar founding member of the group.

"Hello Sergio," she said. "Good to see you. How have you been?" she asked not really wanting to know.

Nodding, he said loudly over the noise, "Good, good."

"Do you know where I can get a glass of wine?" Lena asked.

"My wife?" He said. "My wife's dead."

"Oh. Huh." For a moment, Lena was pensive. She spoke louder in his ear, "So sorry. So, uh, where are the drinks?" He pointed. She went.

A few days later, Lena attended a women's business networking lunch. She became sandwiched between women who had no business sense at all and others who were rough and tough on all levels. Through osmosis, they were all now empowered, connected to and supported by one another. Lena followed up with a woman who said she needed property. The woman never called back. Instead, Lena was continuously called, emailed, and written to by another woman who was hunting her down for charitable donations. Though she was thrilled she gave a prosperous impression, she hoped the stalking would end soon.

28

The following week Lena attended a real estate investors meeting. "Hi, my name is Hen-ry!" Henry was an African American guy who everyone adored. He was entertaining and inspiring.

"I had no education and no money and now I've got 200k in the bank!" Everyone applauded. "If I can do it, you can do it too! Don't be afraid, we're here to help, just ask!" The introductions continued. When it was her turn, Lena said, "I'm Lena," and paused as if in an AA meeting. "And I'm a realtor." Very anticlimactic. Once around the room and the meeting was over. Lots of enthusiasm and motivation. And like an AA meeting, she never saw the attendees again until the next gathering. They continued to remain anonymous.

Continuing on her networking journey, Lena happened into a monthly Chamber event and was immediately bombarded with cards. Hands came at her from all angles. For a moment she imagined she was famous and people wanted her autograph. She collected the cards with one hand, transferred them to the other, and dropped them into the pocket she reserved for discard later.

She made it through the house of cards just in time to greet a bouncy young man who walked up and asked her about her USP. Her what? She opened her mouth to respond, looked at him for a moment, then turned and walked away, leaving the little robot staring blankly, empty head cocked to one side with wide eyes blinking.

She met another young man, almost identical to the first. They seemed to all look alike these days, same outfits, same attitude, same hair purposely cut into a cone-head style. She didn't get it.

"Hi, so my name is Brian. I'm a financial advisor," said young man number two.

"I'm Lena."

"What do you do?"

"I don't know."

"What's your USP?"

Again? What was with these people?

Lena turned away and bumped into an average looking middle aged man with glasses. Kevin looked out through them.

"You lost?" she asked him.

"Kind of. Not sure what to do at these things. I live on the West Coast and am making my way to this side of the state," he replied.

"Try GPS. Or Siri. They know everything. What do you do?"

"I'm a lawyer."

"Hmm."

"What do you do?"

"Haven't committed."

"Me neither. I'm recently divorced."

"I'm sorry?"

"Uncommitted. I'm a staunch Republican."

"What subject are we on?"

"I should tell you that I'm ADD. I have attention deficit disorder. I also have a little OCD, obsessive compulsive disorder. Squirrels."

"Can you take something for it?"

"Yes, I can a little something."

"Please do. "

The rest of the two hours continued to be taxing. Cards kept getting shoved in Lena's face. Newbies on the block kept asking her about her "USP" while they shared their motivational lines, elevator pitches, seminars, and networks that were of little interest. They always began sentences with the word "so," used acronyms and initials rather than the real words, and ended sentences with prepositions. In the old days (she could say this now that she was 50), she simply connected with people who liked her, people she liked, people who could send her business, and people with whom she could do business. No one ever asked what her "USP" was, nor did they care, and they always started sentences and continued conversations with actual meaningful words.

Lena found the young, buzzing, happy piss-and-vinegar types with, heaven forbid, "dreams of the future" simply nerve wracking. Even though she appreciated the ambitions of others, she just didn't care to hear about them. It wasn't the business she was in nor was it any of her business. This networking thing was all about her and it was her time to be the focal point. Why else was she here? And being "all about me" rather than being a people pleaser came well-deserved with age and experience. Perhaps, really, the service industry wasn't for her after all. What else could she do?

She believed that young ones really should only speak when spoken to, and for good reason. They never stopped talking about themselves! Lena was surely much more sophisticated when she was younger. Her focus was always on the other person and how to serve them. In her day, "How to Win Friends and Influence People" was a super read.

Lena was sure that the lack of good listening and communication skills was the base of all evil. People obviously didn't seem to care if she was engaged in the conversation or not. They interrupted or forced their monologue onto her just to hear themselves talk and talk. They could and should do this at home or on a mountain top that echoed. She decided if they were that insistent upon taking over the conversation, she would simply just let them. She tried out this new strategy on the next unsuspecting victim.

One young lady opened and continued a discussion about her goals and aspirations. She went on and on. "I want to be the sole provider of ALF services and by doing so provide the community with well needed care for the aging population...." Lena stopped talking completely. Finally the girl talked herself out without ever asking Lena a single question about herself. Lena stared blankly at the talker until the silence was so uncomfortable the young lady had to suddenly exit to "catch up with Joe."

One of the older guys in the room, a 40-year-old, kept interrupting. Lena countered by talking even more loudly so he would hear her opinion whether he wanted to or not.

A 30-something male kept telling her about his specialty and business. He seemed to know absolutely nothing about everything. She completely tuned him out only to interrupt when she felt like it with whatever was on her mind at the moment, no matter how nonsensical or irrelevant it seemed. "I like green. Yes, that would be the color I would pick," she said in response to the something's comment on the new tires in his shop. These tactics seemed to work better for her. She would participate in a conversation only if she had at least equal time. She did her best to be engaged but really, there was never a conversation that was more interesting than a conversation that was all about her.

She continued to work the room. There was one man who had a loud, deep voice, deeper than James Earl Jones. He kept mumbling. It was distracting. Ironically, the next person Lena ran into was a man who had no voice at all. His voice box had been removed. He was talking with a voice box manipulator. It was a toss-up of which way to go.

Lena sauntered on and met a woman, or a man. She couldn't tell. There literally was nothing to give it away. It was all so confusing.

Then she listened to a lot of people who seemed to be experts on everything, especially in the areas of sports, travel, kids, and food. (Note to self: these topics should be avoided at all costs.) Once people got going on this list, there was no stopping them. Lena knew nothing about sports teams and was exhausted by Achilles heels, torn ligaments, and other sports injuries. People told her what and how it happened, how long it had been, the symptoms, what led them to a doctor and which one, what kinds of treatment they had had over the years, which one worked, which shoes they would use for which exercises they had to do.... And no, she didn't want to see the photo gallery of the trip to the Galapagos years ago or of the kids. Finally, please no more of the dreaded diet talk.

A drink would be good. As Lena headed to the drink line, a man in some kind of *Miami Vice* ensemble with hair slicked up in a cone explained the facts of life to a handful of star-struck women.

"Well, you see, free-range chicken is not actually free range or hormone free," he explained authoritatively, in a voice that reminded Lena of Cliff Clavin from *Cheers*. "The chickens are actually in a larger coop, basically a fenced in space with lots of other angry and freaked out chickens. Then a man in a gas mask comes into the area and stresses the chickens out even more with his presence. The last thing the chicken sees is a butcher knife coming down on her. Of course the constant stress and final shock induces the release of the hormone cortisol, so the chickens actually die with a stockpile of hormones in their system. So, in fact, it is not hormone free and is actually quite the opposite. See what I'm saying?"

Lena nodded with the group. "Oh yeah, totally. Handy information. Something I can really use."

The wine and networking finished, Lena entered an elevator plum worn out. She pushed the down button. Muzak played. She started to bob and weave her head to a song by Michael Jackson. She shimmied. Suddenly she squished her face as if in anguish, threw out her hands like the Lord Jesus on the cross and sang in the worst god awful voice ever, "Thriller, thriller night," continuing the epileptic Tourette's interpretation as she descended. It was quite a release.

And yet, the networking events continued. Cheap wine and horrible appetizers. And more pressed chicken. In ways Lena never thought imaginable, all apparently loaded with hormones. And the entertainment! On the one hand, she thought she would shoot herself if that were her job. On the other hand, it was a job, one more than she had.

29

Lena received an invitation to a VIP networking program via email. That was nice. She made an effort to attend although it was a Friday night and she was exhausted. She had no life so it didn't make a difference. Before going in, she squished and mushed her face to wake up. She entered. She was early and the room was fairly empty, so she checked things out. On the refreshment table, there were pumpkin seeds, carrots, celery, cucumber sticks, olive and tomato spread, avocado spread, and gluten free crackers. Huh.

People began to arrive. They were the worst dressed group Lena had ever seen at a function. She inquired about the alcohol. There was none. Oh no.

And then she found herself in the middle of a multi-level marketing program for some health product line she couldn't pronounce. She was limited in her conversation as everyone was in the same business. They wanted her to be involved. It was the first time in a long time she wasn't being rejected. The attention was actually on her.

"I see hot water, but there are no tea bags," she said.

"Let me see if I can solve that," said a pleasant man who appeared from nowhere.

He left and returned with some sort of small spray can. Pleasant man filled a mug three quarters of the way full with hot water. Taking the can, he sprayed brown liquid from it and filled the mug the rest of the way.

"This can is good for two weeks," he explained. "The coffee is fresh and all natural. Taste it."

"No," said Lena, "I want tea." In order not to appear difficult, Lena told the guy next to her to drink the coffee and he did.

"We don't have tea but we have a power drink that's out of this world. Would you like to try that?" said pleasant man.

"No," responded Lena. "I'll just have water."

The woman next to her laughed a lot. The laugh had a pitch that made Lena's eyes water and squint. Lena really needed a drink and some food. She longed for pressed chicken with hormones.

She quietly meandered out the door and headed to the ladies room, passing a woman on the way in. "Save yourself," she said to the woman as she walked by.

When she was sure no one was looking, Lena changed directions. She entered another conference room where another networking event was being held. She was there, so what the heck. They had alcohol, she knew no one, and she needed to leave with a contact or two. It was doable. Maybe she would meet a silent man who had hobbies.

"Name?" inquired the woman at the check-in.

"I've been called many things," said Lena.

"I'm sorry?"

"Me too. In so many ways. Lena Gorman. I'm preregistered."

The woman at the desk looked through her papers in order to find Lena's registration.

"Well surely you have my name tag," said Lena, noticing the sponsor's sign on the wall. "I'm a guest of Florida Power and Light," she added.

"Oh in that case, just drop a card in the bowl and enjoy. You're good."

"Why yes, I AM good. And happy to be part of the sponsoring team."

As Lena entered, she was quickly greeted by a cheery man, or maybe it was a woman. She was having a hard time figuring it all out these days.

"Hello."

"Hi."

"Your first time here?"

"Yep. And I have a good attitude."

"A virgin! Fab-u-lous! Come over here, grab a drink, and join the lip sync contest. We have tuna tacos."

"Tuna tacos, Lip Sync, Wow!"

Lena was at a gay transsexual party. She couldn't tell which women were born female and which were made, and she supposed that was a good thing. She felt happy and welcomed. Her phone rang. It was Susan.

"Where are you?" Susan asked.

"Well, I was at the worst VIP party ever. It's a multi-level marketing program for some health product line I can't pronounce. I want pressed chicken with hormones and alcohol."

"Maybe you'll meet some nice things, uh, people."

"No, no I won't. They're crazy and poorly dressed. It's a cult I tell you. They serve coffee from a spray can and vegetables. I'm next door now at another party where there's Tuna tacos and alcohol. Lots of people. Just need two contacts."

"Don't be rude. What about your diet?"

"I'm never rude. I had my twigs already."

"You're always rude."

"I'm 50. I'm at a gay transsexual networking social. I don't know who is what. This is the first time my own ambiguity works to my advantage and I want to enjoy every moment. And with Lip Sync! Best event of the year! Can't wait to meet my leads. Bye."

30

Lena spiced up her networking agenda to include an international business function where she met a group of Macedonians. She liked the fact that they had a long, interesting history and loved America as much as she did. She was greeted at the door by a man.

"Come, come in. Have some wine," he said.

"I love you people," she said.

"Have you ever had Rakija?"

"Uh oh. What is it? "

"Macedonian moonshine. Do you know what your name is in Macedonia?"

"I love you even more. I'm pretty sure my name is the same all around the world. It's on my passport."

"Lanita, that's what it is." Lena starts to move to the music.

"Seems like you're a good dancer."

"My gym instructor prays for me."

"You know there are only two people in the world that are chosen. The Jews and the Macedonians. It says so in the Bible and on Facebook."

"Then it must be true. How did you know I was Jewish?"

"You have that look."

"Brown eyes and brown hair?"

"We'll go with that."

"I'm told we all look alike. And apparently we all know each other too."

Lena struck up a conversation with Danita, who made sure she had an endless supply of wine and Rakija. Danita was a Macedonian immigrant who had spent half her life under communist rule. She had common sense and was grounded in practicality. She offered Lena a sense of stability and reality that she would need to make it through tough times.

That night they talked for hours, and they would continue to be friends. Lena confided information about her situation and lawsuit. With an Eastern European accent and dramatic hand gestures Danita commanded, "Don't waste your time in a suit. Who are these people? They are nothing. You, you will always be something. They, they will stay the same." They drank and danced to Macedonian folk music. That was fun too.

"This is the best bar mitzvah I've ever been to," slurred Lena as she got up to dance the hora. Everyone else did another dance.

31

The next day, Lena left a house showing to attend a political fund raiser. Who was she kidding?

She was dressed in casual attire and had to change into something more suitable. She didn't have time to go home so she had to change in the car. She parked in the only place she could find, right in front of the corporate center. She made interesting moves and ducked from passersby. Who would have ever thought she'd be taking off her clothes in a car with no sex involved at age 50? Nothing to selfie home about.

As she approached the sophisticated building's entranceway, Lena made adjustments to straighten herself out. Entering, she engaged herself in conversation to prep for the function.

"Oh beautiful wise one. We have a bit of a hangover but you are still so lovely and smart. I can make deals and money in any situation. I deserve and appreciate more, more, more things," she said, trying to untangle her glasses from her hair.

Others watched.

Lena arrived at the check in.

"Name?" asked a stern woman.

"They call me special."

"What?"

"Lena Gorman."

"Wear this and vote on Tuesday." The woman handed Lena a tee shirt.

"It's what I live and long for," she said.

Lena strolled to the refreshment table and greeted people on the way. "Hello, how are you?" Being the friendly greeter was an unusual role for her to play these days.

At the food table, Lean picked up a paper plate, napkin, and plastic fork. She started to fill her plate. People were singing the National Anthem. Those who didn't know the words sang using other words they just made up, or simply mouthed along. Lena sang another song to the same tune.

"Lena!" bellowed a loud, short woman. Startled, Lena almost dropped her plate.

"Hi Sheila, what's up?"

"What's up? What's up? You're kidding right?"

"Sorry?"

Sheila cornered Lena and pushed her up against the food table. The woman talked at her, waving a finger. She preached about the Federal government controlling local environmental and building guidelines. Another thing to learn.

"Horrific I tell you. Just horrific!"

"Well…. Yes…. Agreed."

"Do you know what this means?"

"Maybe?"

Lena began to eat from the pile of food on her plate.

Sheila moved closer, animated. She continued to wag her finger.

"It means the federal government can control everything on the local level down to what you want to do with your house. You can be fined however much they want for whatever violation they chose."

Lena became anxious. Sweat started to emerge. She piled more food on her plate and into her mouth. She worked around the wagging finger and tried to cover up the food from spittle. She remained fixated on the woman's mouth. It just kept moving. There was no "edit" or "stop" button. Lena's hands worked feverishly between hovering over her food and stuffing her face.

"What does the federal government know about local issues? You have no control because you vote on the local level for local issues, but if you don't do what the EPA wants you to do in your own back yard even though it's okay with the local government, you're screwed!"

Finally, Sheila suddenly stopped talking and looked at Lena. "So," she said, "what you're doing, ya making a living?" Lena was in tears. She paused in mid bite.

Miserable and sweating, Lena wasn't sure. There didn't seem to be any logic, consistency, or efficiency in what she was doing. Real estate was the hardest job she had ever done. Aside from that, she still couldn't commit to the fact she was out of the PR game and that her one opportunity to make it big, quickly, was gone.

She wondered if in fact she could keep up long enough to make a living. Her schedule changed daily. She had to be a prepared expert on everything: the building's structure, code, neighborhood, comparables, market, and more. Now she had to incorporate new Federal guidelines and changes. It was really too much. Real estate was not just about making a deal. It was about making the deal happen in every way, shape, and form. On top of that, she was completely dependent upon outside forces and had no control over anything. She explained it all in her journal.

Lena needed to network in the big leagues. There were some prestigious events that she did in fact want to attend. However, she couldn't afford them. These were events where the upper echelon schmoozed. She herself was once part of the group and she needed to get back to it if she really wanted to build her real estate empire. How was she going to get in? She tried to crash one but her wild hair and off-putting attitude tipped everyone off.

Some suggested that she volunteer. Unbelievable. She would have to be an unpaid worker in places where she once had been honored and connected with on a high level. She would provide free service to more people, but this time to those who formerly worked, networked, and socialized with her. Crap.

She gave it a shot. When she entered a high fluting conference, she was given a t-shirt and badge. She was now branded "volunteer." No one could mistake it; she was a service worker. She recognized people immediately and ducked. She saw the volunteer coordinator and ducked again. She didn't want any assignments and didn't want to work.

She ducked behind commercial vendors. She ducked behind caterers. She ducked some more until she finally ran out of ducking space. At that point, there was no way of avoiding it, she ran smack into someone she knew.

"Lena, I thought I might see you. Where are you sitting?"

"I haven't decided yet."

"Are you involved with the show?"

"Yes, in fact, it's one of my projects," she promptly misrepresented. "I'm not sure I'll have a chance to sit still but I definitely want to catch up at the networking functions if I'm not too busy." Just then the volunteer coordinator came around the corner.

"I'm sorry," she said, "I have to run to the ladies room. Will you excuse me? I'll catch up with you later." With that, Lena ran into the bathroom and played with the faucets until enough time passed where she was sure she wouldn't be noticed or given assignments. This was a disaster. She slipped out quietly and drove home.

Here she was, networking and volunteering at 50. Ugh. Lena noticed that something happened when people turned 50 - at least it did with her. They suddenly got very angry, very quickly, or they instantly became overwhelmed. It was as though the whole world had shifted. Comfort levels just weren't there anymore. Most people needed meds, some more than others. She found that working out, drinking less coffee and eating right all helped, despite the fact that she was continuously on the verge of a nervous breakdown, tears, red hot anger, despair, and pure irrational elation. She had absolutely no patience for people and things that wasted her time.

No it wasn't "the change." Nor were the hot and cold sweats she had at night, during meetings, and at networking events. It was all the other changes that couldn't be controlled that drove her over the edge. She carried on in more ways than one.

Rounding out her networking excursions were a hemp fest and an orthodox wedding. She figured that she could meet a man or make a business contacts at either one. At the hemp fest she marveled at the great new design and glass industries. There were activities, string, clothes, and bongs that looked like phalluses. One booth gave little ones away for free. Lena took three.

The orthodox wedding was a good time. Lots of dancing and lots and lots of speeches. She sat next to the grandmother of the bride who said rather blandly, "Look what I started."

"More water?" Lena asked.

"Why should I have water when I can have wine?" she answered. The woman said she needed it to make it through all the "Mazel Tovs" and introductions to people she didn't know or care about. Lena's kind of woman.

32

Lena met up with Susan to powerwalk. After Lena delivered her daily monologue of activities and complaints, Susan asked, "You know you're in the service industry, right?" Susan was particularly intuitive today and on high perspective alert.

Typically before they crossed any road, she made sure all the cars were off the street. Lena always ran into traffic. Today, Susan surprised Lena by crossing while cars were still in view.

"Susan, did you do that all by yourself?" inquired a surprised Lena.

A proud Susan replied, "Why yes, yes, I did."

"Good for you. Let's do that again sometime." She was relieved at least something was actually moving along.

They took a break for lunch at a quick-serve Mexican eatery. They got in line. With food in hand, Lena tried to grab the only remaining seats. An older woman with an accent told her the seats were reserved. Susan was appalled.

"They're breaking the system. When you hold up seats, you ruin the flow. People are supposed to get their food, sit, eat, and leave. If you take the seats before you have the food, you slow down the process. People won't be able to sit, eat, and move as quickly." See, 50. Change.

Lena would think about this from now on. It was important that she learn.

"So I met a guy," said Lena.

"You met a guy?"

"Well, yes, not so out of the realm of possibilities."

"What's he like?"

"He's got ADD and OCD and is a JD."

"Quite an abbreviated individual. Another attorney. You like him?"

"I don't know. We can talk about everything as long as the conversation changes every 90 seconds. He's clean though."

"Well, that's something. Does he make you laugh?"

"Yes, he's not serious about anything."

"What do you talk about?"

"Politics, sailing, finance, politics, sailing, finance, life, work, sailing, every couple of minutes. It's hard to keep up. It's exhausting actually."

"Hmm, well, let's see how that works out."

33

Back at her home office, Lena delved into residential real estate. Her new client Jose was in a wheel chair, the result of a car accident. He had a steady business as an agent for up and coming musicians. He was busy. To him, there was no such thing as a handicap.

The only limit Jose had was that he could only afford to spend up to a certain amount. He had very specific ideas of what he wanted for $150,000. These included three bedrooms, two bathrooms, a pool, and a huge backyard with a total of 10,000 square feet. He didn't care what shape the house was in. He and his family would fix it up. Lena thought his focus would make her job easier. Hardly. She failed miserably. He was grateful she tried.

Next she had a client who wanted a house that cost between sixty and seventy thousand. She didn't know of any.

Then there was a client who didn't know whether or not she would be qualified for a mortgage. She thought she probably could swing $125,000 but would only look at $250,000 houses. She wanted to buy right away.

Then she had a client who was blind.

One of her clients was a woman who had made her money in the fashion industry. She was 75. She once had a nice fortune of eight million dollars. Little by little she lost it through bad experiences she refused to discuss. Lena, of course, had to know. Perhaps she was a kindred spirit. The ex-multi-millionaire showed her photos and memorabilia of a glamorous past. Lena was intrigued and enjoyed the history. The woman begged Lena to sell her last few remaining pieces of land. She had cancer and needed the money. Lena was moved. She told the universe she was grateful for time and health and vowed to use both wisely.

Another client was very religious. She had been displaced due to an eminent domain project and was now living with her aging mother. She played the guitar and talked a lot. She had Lupus and a sister who had just died of cancer. Lena wondered what the funeral was like. Should she mention she did funeral work as well? For anything that may come up with the mom and all in the near future?

On top of everything else, the woman was also overwhelmed with legal deadlines in her job as an attorney. First she wanted an office. Then she wanted an office and a house. Then she wanted a virtual office and a house. Then she wanted an office in a house. Then she didn't know what to do. After Lena had spent a full day listening to everything about everything, the woman decided to do nothing about anything. She announced she would remain with her mother and put her office inside their home.

To focus her efforts and be more efficient, Lena's broker suggested a practice known as "farming." This phenomenon allowed a realtor to become specialized in a certain geographical area. Farming realtors worked only their chosen areas. They studied and knew everything and anything about them. They presented themselves as resident experts. They marketed and branded with the area. It was "theirs." Any competition would be viciously and furiously attacked. But she didn't know what to wear for such specialized work. Pantyhose, practical shoes? Loose shirts? She mostly dressed for comfort these days.

Lena wasn't a farmer. She was a realtor without a home, without direction. She ran all over three counties because, well, she wasn't that bright. Life didn't get easier for her because somehow she always made it as difficult as possible. Pain is gain, as they say in the gym. And so far, it's been all pain. She aimed to streamline better. She hoped to begin that process soon. Step Seven. She began researching possible farming niches. The one with cemetery plots held the most potential. Worth considering.

34

Lena awoke to another day in the life of a realtor. She looked at herself in the mirror. Not much had changed. She still looked like a madwoman. She still hoped it was all a dream. She still hadn't found a rhythm to her new life yet. She didn't have a clue as to what she would be doing that day, the rest of the week, or the rest of her life for that matter.

She worked out at 6 a.m., got on the computer at 7:30, and then reviewed her emails one by one. She deleted, deleted, deleted, read, responded, read, responded, read, responded, and searched for properties. She sent out property options immediately via email so that her eager beavers and demanding clients would have them at the start of their day. The process made her appear super organized and concerned for their well-being. After her breakfast break, she continued to search, send, and set up appointments. A couple of disrespectful clients would unfortunately respond immediately. The nerve. This interrupted her flow and peace of mind. Though she was up early, she certainly couldn't and didn't want to talk before 9 a.m. What was the rush?

Then, there were showings. Unplanned and on demand. Preparing for a showing was a challenge. Lena would confirm the time, date, availability, and showing instructions over and over again. If she would be showing several places at a time, she had to schedule it just right. She chased down listing agents. Sometimes this took hours. Once she communicated with the agent, the agent had to check with the owner and maybe a tenant. Then the agent would get back to her. Sometimes the showing was set and then cancelled. Then reset and cancelled again. Still the other side might not cooperate and she would have to start all over again. After a series of texts, calls and emails, a showing finally would be securely scheduled.

Once that was done, there were preparations to be made. Lena printed out the listing and all the relevant information on the properties, double checked lockbox and supra codes when applicable, reviewed instructions, checked directions and addresses, and made notes. It was anyone's guess as to whether or not she would be able to read them later given her handwriting.

In the midst of all this, and much to her dismay, her attorney called, several times. The brothers had opposed the latest motion. There were changes to be made and they fought over everything. There would be yet another hearing.

35

Showings meant Lena had to decide what to wear in public. At her home office, she rarely got out of her pajamas before late afternoon. Real estate had no dress code. South Florida had no particular style other than bad. It seemed no one appreciated pantyhose anymore. She tried wearing suits for a while but sweated heavily at showings. She tried early morning showings, but that didn't help. Little by little, she discarded her suits and pantyhose and learned to dress SoFla casual and comfortable. She was finally able to blend.

Within months, however, Lena took it a step further. This new-found dress freedom allowed her to let it all hang out. She wore wrinkled shirts and barely applied makeup. Her collection of accessories helped to cover up sore spots and food stains and, on occasion, to add accent. Her hair was whatever it intended to be that day. Sometimes she forgot to comb it. She often went out with shoes that didn't match and explained it was a new French look. She was pretty much a mess and wondered if anyone noticed. She was unraveling.

It took a while, but finally Lena began to sort herself out. She combed her hair and became creative with scarves. With a decent shirt and slacks, one could wrap a scarf, and voila! Just like that she looked like a professional. Makeup and jewelry were musts at her age. She knew her limitations.

36

Directions and driving. Another challenge. Though there was a space for directions on the listing, most realtors annoyingly left it blank. Lena was terrible with directions, and she was worse at driving. While she was eating, reading, putting on makeup, phone dialing, texting, talking, and doing research, other cars travelled around her. Since the bulk of the data she had was in the cellphone, it was always interesting when people called for information. It was even more fun when there was a bad connection or a disconnect.

Lena fought traffic and slow drivers when it rained. Tourists stopped in the middle of the road without warning or reason. When people signaled left and turned right it annoyed her. She had road rage daily. It caused her mouth to spew obscenities.

As she pulled up to a light, she looked to her right and saw a sign that said, "Life Extension Expansion Center." Aside from it being redundant, she had no idea what it meant. She never thought about extending and expanding her life, or both at the same time.

The car on her left jammed and rocked to the day's hip hop. The sound was driving her crazy. She signaled the other driver to roll down his window. First she motioned with the old fashioned circular motion gestures. He was too young to understand. Then she pointed to her window and made it go up and down up and down for show and tell. The kid finally got it. He rolled down his window. Lena said, "Yes, hi, how are ya? Listen, can you please change the station? Something like the greatest hits from the 80s and 90s or Lite 101.3? I really need to center my mind, body, and soul."

The driver and his friends looked at her blankly and drove off leaving a straight view of another sign that bemused her. "Dental Dentures" it read. What other kind is there? Honestly.

The light turned green and Lena prayed she wouldn't get lost. The pressure was intense. South Florida streets had no rhyme or reason and sometimes her GPS and Google maps couldn't find her. Other times, they took her on a journey through site and sound only to take her back to the same spot via north, south, east, and west. When her phone rang the directions continued in her ear and she got even more confused. When the screen or colors changed, she was beside herself. The "Twilight Zone" theme played in her head and she took deep labor breaths to calm down. "Oh God, Oh God, Oh God." The words "lost satellite" caused grave panic, but when she heard "You have arrived," as she slammed on the brakes and hit a garbage can, she replied "Why yes, yes I have." She hopped out of the car and tried to look in control. She had crumbs on her face and coffee stained papers in hand. "Beat that," she said proudly. Then she burped.

37

Lena often met her clients for the first time at the door or gate of the property she was showing. It made her very anxious. Sometimes the gatekeeper wouldn't let her in or the lock boxes didn't work. There were two kinds. The standard combo lock was easier and cheaper to use. However, sometimes the realtor gave the wrong code, often confusing the number and letters on the boxes. She'd call from the site and wait with her clients until the heat of the sun finally forced them all to discard pieces of clothing and eventually part ways. The Supra lock came with or without codes, an application she had to install on her phone, a fob, a pin number, and a monthly fee. Having an extra anything was a nightmare for Lena. She had already lost two fobs.

During a showing, Lena would overstate the obvious. She tried to hide the fact that she knew absolutely nothing about décor or structure, whether it was frame, CBS, or block construction. She had no vision for these things and knew it. "Look," she said of the wallpaper with her best Fosse hand gestures. "It's blue! And what a lovely shade it is. And this, this corner cabinet, great use of space." She skipped ahead to point things out before the buyers got to them. "Look, windows that go out. And a walk-in closet." Or, "just look at this old Florida tile, how quaint. And here... this...." She just simply couldn't remember the word and used hands to finish the description. And then there were some things that just simply were indescribable.

One client had a lazy eye, and Lena didn't know which one to look at.

Lena agreed with everything the client said and guessed at some answers.

She entertained and discussed refrigerators, a/c units, pools and land-scaping, roofs, windows, bathrooms, whatever, all things she knew noth-ing about. Rinse and repeat, over and over again.

She made sure she had specific information from the multiple listing service, a.k.a. MLS along with other information she prepared ahead of time, but then she wouldn't be able to find her glasses, and her continual squinting was useless. She tried to fake it from memory, but didn't have much left. Sometimes she would fudge a few answers and have to come back with correct ones.

38

Lena felt that a realtor hadn't seen anything until he or she had been doing showings for at least a year. The process was a real cultural learning experience. Houses ranged from garish to tasteful, from Italian Classic to Caribbean to Eastern European to sleek minimalist. Whatever she seemed to find tasteful, elegant and lovely, her clients couldn't wait to change.

Showings also kept Lena informed about the newest styles of home design and up to date on what was "out there." Of course, it was all subjective. In some places, she appreciated the design. In others, she had to vacate the premise immediately or she'd jump out of her skin.

She was always intrigued by the state of a house as well, whether it was a total mess with lots of abuse or a happy homemaker special. Each place offered a feast of sights and colors! She realized she had never made her own house into a home. The more she saw others, the more she appreciated her own real estate. She was ashamed she had done nothing to keep it up, even back when she had the money. There was no excuse for laissez faire décor.

How did all these people have so much vision? She couldn't even decide on a lightbulb. There were so many choices in styles and wattages. In her place, everything was original, exactly the way it was when she bought it 14 years ago. It was a bit of a concern. Especially since all the appliances were breaking down and her toaster oven caught on fire. Though that might have nothing to do with her interior design skills, it was still something she had to think about.

Lena also considered the lives that were led in these homes. She began to notice the knickknacks, the colors, the way pictures were hung and their subjects, the way the landscaping was laid and the grass was cut, the way the bathroom was set up and the kitchen was coordinated. She observed the many different kinds of Jesus portraits and tried to figure out which one was the most correct.

She imagined for a minute what it would be like to have lived in this house or that one. What types of things did the inhabitants do on a daily basis? What kinds of lives did they lead? Did they appreciate their good fortune? Were they moving on to better pastures? Did they get kicked out, divorced, or lose a job? That would be horrible. Still, she wanted to know the dirt. She had an inquiring mind.

39

Lena believed in good karma and Feng Shui. She got a feeling when she walked into a house. If it felt good, she felt great about presenting it. Other times she ran for her life. Either it was really disgusting or very high end, which made her insanely jealous.

Some properties were a total disaster. Lena couldn't understand how anyone could punch a wall, pull out the ceiling, leave roof leaks, live in mildew, and let a place go. Even she had her limits. How could anyone take a good house and rip it to shreds, leaving only remnants of quality construction including custom build outs and crown molding? It was unconscionable. If someone owned something, they should care for it. If that weren't bad enough, sellers often priced their properties at market value rather than true value. Lena told one seller he should try living in his property for a few days and get back to her.

Lena was never comfortable showing major fixer uppers. In general, she didn't touch door knobs or anything in the kitchen or bathrooms. She worried about hazards, workman's compensation, and disinfecting herself throughout the day. She wondered why she hadn't brought a face mask.

If she had to lift the tiny light lever or touch anything, she covered her hands with her sleeves or used the paper towels and gloves she learned to bring with her. She knew that germs and mold were lethal and wondered if she could get Ebola from a wall. She watched the roaches and ants scurry. Why God, why?

When things were incredibly beautiful and well laid out, Lena was in heaven. A well-appointed home with hand-picked decorative items carefully presented along with the fine furniture was utopia. Everything cared for and elegant made her swoon. She could feel the money dripping from the chandeliers. She hugged the walls. Even though it was not her taste, she enjoyed walking into these properties pretending she was the buyer. She touched and felt things to really appreciate the exquisite beauty. She left fingerprints everywhere.

Meanwhile, Lena had to deal with reality and prepare for more court hearings. The brothers were now coming up with new arguments that made no sense, keeping her in litigation, themselves in business, and the lawyers well compensated. She didn't even know what the argument du jour was, but her attorney kept saying it was not a big deal. He could, of course, afford to say that.

40

There were three options when showing a property. It could be a tenant-occupied, owner-occupied or vacant property. Of course, vacant was ideal. When a property had a tenant or owner still living on the premises, Lena and her clients were distracted by smells, sloppiness, personal items, decorating, and/or the people themselves.

Rental properties with the tenants present were uncomfortable, especially when Lena and her clients were being followed. Some tenants were resentful they had to go through "all" this. They worried that the new owners would kick them out. Some made Lena and her clients feel as though they were invading their personal space. Others really wanted to get involved in the showing. Even if they didn't speak the same language, they were determined to show off the salient features of the property anyway. Some simply liked the company and would talk as long as allowed. Others wanted to meet the potential new owner in the hopes of being allowed to remain in the property. The situation always added another dimension of stress to the showing.

The real nightmare was conducting a showing with an unmotivated but had-to-sell owner present. The state of the place and the owner's attitude depended upon what had happened to push the sale. It could be the result of a divorce, a foreclosure, a short sale, an estate sale, or any number of very unpleasant life happenings. If it were a foreclosure, short sale, or divorce, the place would be a mess and the owner would be grouchy. With an estate sale as a result of a death, everything would be neat and nicely arranged for sentimental and respectful reasons, but then the owner usually was more reluctant to sell for the same reasons.

A showing with a motivated owner present was better because there was more control over the situation. Why just the other day she had the good fortune of working with one such owner. She coordinated a showing with a repeat client and met him at the property. She opened the lockbox and door with ease. On the other side of the door, in the middle of the living room, there stood a naked man. She felt bad in so many ways. She apologized profusely to the owner and to her client. After he dressed, the owner gave a great presentation of the property, better than she ever would have. He was very nice and extremely thorough, pointing out all the upgrades and amenities. He didn't have much to hide at that point. He seemed to be well connected, as the autographed photos of presidents and astronauts suggested. It was a very pleasant showing in a beautiful condo. Naturally, her client wanted something else.

Always Lena hoped the tenants or owners would be out and the place would be tidy. She also prayed there were no animals present. All potential buyers seemed to be terrified of animals. The smaller the animal, the worse it was. Small dogs made messes everywhere, barked the whole time, and snapped at her. For some reason, they always snapped at her. And rodents inevitably got loose, creating even more entertainment. A showing with a cat could be just as much fun. So many people seemed to be allergic to cats. Others just hated them, especially when they darted here and there just to annoy or trip the client.

41

In order to sell more, Lena realized that she needed to get a better feel for her clients' interests and motivations. Step Eight. As she showed potential buyers around she began to watch their expressions and movements, carefully observing what was catching their eye. As if on cue, she would make a comment about something they clearly were contemplating. She eavesdropped on every conversation and followed and led them around. Some found her espionage unnerving.

She became cognizant of the relationships among her clients. She was perceptive as to all the nuances based on her experience with her own dysfunctional family. It was worse when her clients were people she knew. Then she was more intimately involved than she wished to be. She really didn't want to know people any better than she already did and certainly never wanted to get involved in their personal relationships. Despite her best efforts and much to her chagrin, Lena often found herself in the middle of private issues.

A friend of hers, Sandra, wanted to buy a house. Her new boyfriend Mike was along for the ride to add perspective and be helpful. He didn't and wasn't. Most of the time, he spewed negative comments like pea soup in *The Exorcist*. The air was thick with tension. Armed as a professional would be, Lena stayed on task and presented several properties for discussion. They made a date to see some of them.

To begin, they looked at a small, cluttered, green house. There were three grown children selling the house. They had a widowed mother in a nursing home. This was her house, and the family needed the funds to care for her. Lena put in an offer for the couple. First, the family wanted the full asking price. Then there was a competitive cash offer for less than the asking price that came under consideration. After all, cash is always king in real estate. Then the owners decided they needed more money to subsidize the mother's care. But, as it turned out, she was fully covered under Medicaid. As luck would have it, the other buyer disappeared after the sellers insisted on the full asking price. Although Lena and her clients were the last offer standing, the owners suddenly stopped returning calls and counters and abruptly ended all negotiations.

Weary, Lena and her clients moved on. They found a sprawling ranch house full of a dead lady's clothes. The sprawling ranch was nice, with a big walkout patio area that Lena herself found attractive. The woman who owned the house had died from cancer a year ago. Her daughter lived across the street and maintained the house with all of its possessions just as her mom had left it. Food was still in the refrigerator, clothes still hanging in the closet, trash still trashy. Still, Lena and her clients put in an offer. There was no response. Lena and the other realtor communicated frequently. Finally, the daughter's realtor, in a fit of anger exclaimed, "the fucking fat bitch won't give me an answer" and something about the fact that he hated that fat bitch. She sure must be fat. Lena pointed out to her clients that perhaps the daughter might not be the best neighbor to have, and the realtor obviously had a few issues of his own.

Next, they checked out a story-book castle house. The little castle was a real brick Tudor style home, lovely from the road and well-maintained on three acres of beautiful land. The tax bill on the land was more than that on the house. They discussed the possibility of selling off the back acre as others had done in the past, but unfortunately zoning no longer allowed it. The boyfriend thought there were strong possibilities of using the land to produce income in other ways. He was so excited he used the photo of the house as his computer wallpaper.

The house was in good shape and sported a very efficient a/c unit. The kitchen was the only sore spot. The seller offered a small incentive to assist. It was the most expensive property they had considered thus far, and they loved it. They put in an offer for full price. Much to their surprise and disappointment, the owners accepted a cash offer from someone else. All were angry and bitter, bitter, bitter.

Sandra was stuck. She needed to move, sign a temporary and possibly more expensive lease, or maybe a yearly lease. After some consideration, she chose to stay put and sign a three-month lease. This was costly to her, and the pressure was percolating.

A couple of days later, Mike drove through another neighborhood and saw a house he liked. Unbeknownst to Lena, Sandra and Mike went to check it out. The sellers were facing foreclosure and working on a short sale. A previous buyer fell through, so it was possible that the short sale might not take a year. The mother and son owners were a little nutty and sad. Still, they kept impeccable house repair and utility service records. They made terrific improvements that presented an overall good impression. The only downside was some water in the basement. Sandra and Mike made an offer directly, without Lena. In the meantime, Lena kept researching properties for them in the hopes of finding the perfect dream home for her friends. After much effort, she found one and called the couple immediately.

"Sandra, I hope you like some of the ideas I sent. Today I found the perfect one! What's your schedule?"

"We just signed a deal," said Sandra.

"What?"

"Mike drove by a place yesterday and called the number. We put in an offer, they accepted, and we close in 30 days. Isn't that wonderful?"

"Yes….Yes it is. I'm so happy for you. Did you let them know you had a realtor?"

"No need. It's an estate sale and there's a lawyer."

"The lawyer works for the seller and gets a commission. Both sides of the commission are being paid regardless. The only difference is that since you called directly, you would have to specify that I am included as your realtor and that you have an agreement."

"Well...."

"It doesn't cost anyone anything extra and I make sure your best interests are continuously taken care of with the contract and follow-up work. It's a win-win."

"We're okay. You didn't find us this house so it's kind of weird now. I don't want to rock the boat."

"Sandra this is how I get compensated for my time. It's totally free to you and makes no difference in the processing or the price. It's okay for the client to also bring a property to the realtor, but to be cut out after working together is not right. We've known each other for years."

"Lena, let's just leave it. I really appreciate your time. Let's get together again soon. Thanks."

Sandra hung up. Lena stared at her phone.

The short sale went through. The house closed in six weeks. There was only one month of double bills with Sandra's lease. The extra time allowed Sandra to move at her own pace with as little stress as possible. There was enough time to go in, paint, and redo the floors. Mike painted the purple garage door white and the purple front door "Red Door Red." They were happy.

Lena watched as her friends moved on with their lives while hers remained stagnant and spiraling downward. Her industry colleagues told her, "Buyers are liars and no one is loyal."

Lena received a new referral that seemed easy enough. Cathy was a middle aged woman looking for a condo for her friend. It was a nice story. Cathy was going to put money down to help her long-time friend Charlie who had no money but did a have a job. He was over 55 and qualified for senior housing.

Lena showed several condos almost daily over the course of a month. Cathy couldn't make a decision and was demanding in more ways than one. She had no car, so Lena had to pick her up and drive her around. Then Cathy didn't like Lena's driving and was terrified of everything on the road. Then she was too hot; then she was too cold. She often didn't feel well. On one occasion her low blood sugar kicked in and they had to stop at a grocery store. Instead of stopping for a quick pick-up to offset the sudden drop in blood sugar levels, Cathy decided to take advantage of the opportunity to do some grocery shopping while Lena stayed in the car waiting. Upon returning to the car a half hour later, Cathy asked Lena to pop the trunk for her groceries.

"You went shopping?" Lena asked.

"Yes, I hope you don't mind. I figured while I was here, why not," said Cathy.

"Indeed."

With anger boiling, Lena watched Cathy put her groceries into the car. Cathy got in and they drove off.

"Aren't you going to eat something?" Lena asked.

"No. I feel better just knowing the food is around in case I really need it."

Lena's violent visions returned with a vengeance.

After the month was over, it turned out that Charlie was not qualified and couldn't afford anything. Cathy couldn't help after all. So, there went the project along with a huge chunk of lost time.

As life is circular, they came back. After a few months, Lena received a call from Cathy saying that Charlie was now qualified, so they could go out and look for condos again. Just as soon as they found one, the mortgage company said that no, in fact Charlie was not qualified for condos because he couldn't afford the maintenance fees. He could, however, get a townhouse or a single family home under a hundred thousand dollars.

Still Cathy called daily regarding condos. Lena reminded her that the buyer was not qualified. After some time, the reality clicked in for Cathy and she had her husband sign up as the second buyer. Now they could afford to buy. Even more exiting, they could continue the search.

Lena found Cathy property after property. Months later, they were still looking. Goldilocks couldn't settle into something and Lena was beside herself. She received calls night and day on the same topics over and over again and still, nothing. More often than not, Cathy just stayed on the phone long after the conversation ended, and Lena couldn't figure out why they were still chatting. Finally she talked Cathy into putting in offers to get the ball rolling. One was actually accepted, but then it didn't appraise high enough. Another was executed after that, but then the association wanted six months of fees in advance, and that wasn't going to work.

Finally, Lena gave up. She tried to give Cathy away to another realtor, but no one would take her. Cathy didn't want to go.

"You're not only my realtor, you're my friend."

Lena normally would be moved by such a statement, but she just didn't see how this relationship was either friendly or a benefit to her.

42

Clients continued to call all day and all night. She had to be available as she was a realtor and had no life aside from serving them. By early evening, she already had a list of assignments of wants and needs for the next day and could barely stay awake. There were always wants and needs. Lots of them.

When Lena was really lucky, she would get a call about some issue that caused high anxiety for her client. Evidently, it was her job to solve every problem and provide advice on irrelevant topics. Lena was surprised at how many people shared their most intimate details with people they just met. Her world was becoming a stage and all the people merely players - all with their own monologues and private audiences.

Lena became overwhelmed with information and issues, constant correspondence, a schedule that continued to be out of control, and more bills that remained unopened. She received an infinite number of emails, texts, and calls, sometimes from people she hadn't met about something she couldn't remember. She started drinking coffee again. All the people she met in networking and on the road wanted to "follow up" and "have coffee." She was up to six cups a day.

Her cats were getting antsy and even more bizarre. They wanted in, then they wanted out, in, then out, and she had no cat door.

Rubber bands and plastic bags kept multiplying. She had no idea how.

The lawsuit never seemed to have an end in sight. There were the hearings, the prep work for the hearings, the lack of control, the wondering and stressing over how it would all turn out, the expense, the anger, and the bitterness. Would there ever be a conclusion to the madness? The settlement wasn't settled, the judgment was still pending, and in between she continued to be told she was all wrong.

On top of that, she lost her sunglasses, reading glasses, keys, papers, and mind. When she lost the calculator, she screamed. When she lost her remote, she sobbed, "Why, Oh God, why?" When she lost a client file and couldn't get in touch with the owner about his listing, she almost had a breakdown. How could she work so hard, know so much, have so many calls, increase her responsibilities, and have no money? Moreover, how could anyone have children? "Your call will be answered in the order it was received!" she yelled at the phone.

Lena tried lighting candles to relax. They never seemed to smell as nice as they did in the store. She stared at the gecko her cats gifted to her and wondered how he got in and how she would get him out. She just got through cleaning up bird feathers from a carcass that was mysteriously missing. She didn't know how that happened, but what was outdoors seemed to eventually appear inside in her indoor/outdoor home. She blinked twice. The genie bit didn't work.

After a long day of clients and cats, Lena was tired. If she could summon up enough energy, she watched television. She lived vicariously through the more violent programs. She visualized the defendants in her case being slashed by her: Lena the slasher! Sometimes she visualized her clients as well. She carried these visions to bed with her and throughout the next day. It provided a sense of relief and control.

Sometimes she didn't move from her computer at all. Her head would simply fall hard on the machine as she collapsed from exhaustion into a deep sleep, eyes fluttering, tongue out, snoring. Thing 1 snuggled up next to her head. Thing 2 coughed up a hairball at her feet.

43

Susan called.

"Allo," Lena grunted.

"Wow, rough night?"

"Rough year. I'm so exhausted I can't think straight. Real estate is never ending and the lawsuit is taking up so much time and energy. Every time I move ahead just a little, I get a call that something else is going on. And I'm my own paralegal to boot. I should have gone to law school and became my own attorney. For all the time, effort, and money, I would have had a better new career."

"Just hang in there. You're doing the right thing. And being a lawyer? Really? Try the Sudafed. Gives you a kick and keeps you focused."

"Interesting. And good to know. What part of my life would I be focused on?"

"Take two, I'm telling you it helps with middle age."

"Everyone knows more than me."

Lena took a Jonathan apple off her desk and bit into it.

44

She felt like she was on a treadmill going nowhere. Nothing she was doing was making her enough money or moving her forward despite her best efforts. Compounding her financial problems, the potential leases for her commercial building investment fell by the wayside, leaving her with expenses and no income. Her partner wanted another realtor.

Time passed; Lena struggled. The money flow just wasn't there and she was frustrated with the lack of momentum. She became more and more depressed and stilted in her conversations. She stopped socializing with friends and gave up networking. She let herself go. Her house was a mess and the cats were cranky. She was beginning to look like "Pig Pen" from Charlie Brown. She began eating gluten with icing again. A good night for her was Funyuns, candy, and wine watching "Forensic Files."

She was having physical problems too. Her neck became so stiff from the computer she could barely move. Her chiropractor told her to keep rotating her head. This was after he held her upside down, pinched her neck, cracked her bones, rubbed her with a sonogram, applied electromagnetic shock therapy, and administered alternating ice and heat packs.

Susan came over to see how things were progressing. They sat in the living room. A frog hopped along the floor. They watched it go by. Lena rolled her head.

"So, I'm going to pray over my debt," said Lena matter of factly. "On Good Friday, there's a thing."

"Okay. Couldn't hurt. At least you won't be persecuted for believing in nothing like an Atheist in Bangladesh. Why can't you just get a loan or refinance?"

"Because I don't have steady income. When I had money, it wasn't a problem. It's when I need it, there's a problem. And it gets worse as time goes by."

"Well, I see you're off the diet." Susan ducked and swatted at a fly.

"And now my neck is killing me from the computer. I can't really move too much."

"Would you anyway? Did you go to a... a...."

"No. I did go to a chiropractor. He told me to keep moving my head. See...." Lena pointed at her head. "Moving my head." She bobbled.

"You look like a bubbling bobble head with a twitch."

45

Lena went to meet her father for dinner.

"Pass the bread dear," he said once they were seated at the table. Disheveled, she reached for the bread, took two rolls, and passed the plate to her father. She attacked the rolls. Her father looked at her.

"Yes, I'm eating gluten. So, what of it?"

"You look different."

"Absolutely nothing has changed."

"Have you been out in public?"

"Yes, yes I have. The public is made up of crazy, self-centered, egotistical, mean, wacky people."

"You're the normal one?" He looked at Lena who was a mess, head bobbing and arms twitching.

Her father told her it was time to pull herself together. "I don't care much for this side of you. You're becoming a whirling dervish. And not in a good way. Remember who you are and what's important," he said. Her life as she knew it was gone forever and her debt seemed to be here to stay. Where could she apply this new earth-shattering advice? Step Nine.

46

Perhaps some live spiritual relief and guidance would really help thought Lena. She visited a Temple, hoping to find religion and a way to pray over her debt. As she entered, she realized she was one of only two people from her generation and younger attending the service. A white-haired four-piece band made up of a clarinet, a fiddle, drums, and a keyboard accompanied a woman who donned a low-cut scoop neck dress. Her boobs were up and out. She sang as if in a hotel nightclub with hand and body gestures grooving and moving to ancient Hebrew chants. "Everybody now," she said. The Rabbi played music videos between the prayers. Lena bobbed and weaved. Times sure had changed at Temple.

For added measure and direction, Lena consulted her psychic on the way home. She was told she would receive plenty of money from multiple sources. Money from her lawsuit would come in drips and drabs, and there would be a few job offers. The course of her life would depend on what she wanted and chose. The psychic told her not to worry. She would have lots of money and happiness. She would get a man, travel, and move. Lena was hopeful. Choices again!

On the way home, she stopped and picked up a box of Sudafed. She wanted to cover all the bases.

47

For lack of anything better to do at the moment, Lena continued with research, cold calls, and showings. She met all kinds of people at showings. She tried to be prepared for anything that might happen. Recent news reports on assaults made her nervous, so she began bringing a weapon with her. She knew karate too. What she hadn't prepared for was encountering a gorgeous client. She met him on site, and wow! He was a young, good looking hot-to-trot, up-and-coming professional. Boobs don't fail me now, she thought to herself. She couldn't look at him or remember anything about the property because he was so handsome. She was having trouble walking behind him because he had such a nice butt, so she moved in front and added a little sex strut. When she did this, however, she couldn't seem to remember how to walk. So she talked, and babbled, and talked and babbled, while her head bobbled and her arm twitched. She prayed the showing would end quickly and that he would just make up his mind. Alas, he did not and she had to continue to show him properties throughout the week. Eventually, he bought something and she was thrilled that the tension and threat of her attacking him were finally eliminated. And money! Yes, that was a bonus too.

The following week she had another good meet-up. This time it was with a young Chinese woman. She liked Lu immediately and took her under her wing. Lu wanted to invest in real estate and seemed to have the funds to do it. She was very careful and nervous. She asked all the right questions and did her homework. Lena enjoyed working with her. In a short time, they had narrowed down the list of properties and Lena set up a schedule of showings. While they drove around Lena taught Lu how to sing and dance to American music in the car. Lu became her back-up and harmony. As time went on, Lena and Lu became a great duo singing harmony to such hits as Gladys Knight and Pips, "Leaving on a midnight train to Georgia,," Hall and Oates, "I can't go for that," Bee Gees, "Staying Alive," and of course "Super Freak" by Rick James. When Lena dropped Lu off back at the office where they started, they giggled like little girls as they said goodbye. Gifts from the universe.

48

Lena decided to follow the financials to find higher-end properties she could represent. Maybe that would be her farm. She visited downtown Miami for a presentation on a new building. When she was growing up, Miami had been the place people came to retire or get shot. Either way, they died there.

At that time, South Florida as a whole didn't offer much in the way of big business, entertainment, and culture. Lena never planned on coming back or staying as long as she had. She stayed because of family. Now Miami was a major market to be reckoned with and she wanted a piece of it. Too bad she didn't speak the language. Life was filled with irony.

Lena talked to herself as she walked down the street. "I am one with the universe. The universe will provide. I love and appreciate all things around me. I live life with purpose and passion. I am beautiful." Someone spat as she walked by. "Okay, very nice."

Her phone rang. It was Susan. "Lena, there might be a job opening at CSW. It's perfect for you."

"Shut your mouth! Really? Tell me more," Lena said.

"It's Marketing Director of their government relations department. You'd be able to really take something to the next level."

"You can get me in?" shouted Lena.

"Yes, the woman who had the position dropped dead and now it's open. Isn't that wonderful?" said Susan.

"It's certainly interesting," Lena replied cautiously. "Who's doing her funeral?"

"Doesn't matter how you get in, just get in. Okay, Chow, chow."

Lena hung up and was just about to put her phone in her purse when it rang again.

"Hello, this is Lena."

"Lena, it's David. We need to move faster on this listing. How come the house hasn't sold yet?"

"No one wants it. I don't know why actually. We're posted everywhere and the comps show it's priced right. I really don't understand it myself. Let's give it a couple of more days and consider lowering the price. Can you do that?" asked Lena.

"Possibly. What about an open house?"

"Yes, we could do that. No problem. When do you want to do that?"

"How about next Saturday, midday, 11-2?"

"Sounds good."

They hung up and Lena continued walking, deep in thought. She entered the room where the presentation was being held. She approached a dark man with a stern face. He broke into a smile when he recognized her.

"Hi Ricardo," she said.

"Thank you for coming Lena. I hope we can do some business together," Ricardo answered.

"Me too! Can't wait to see this project. By the way, open houses, ever heard of these?"

Ricardo looked at her, not sure he understood. "I hope you enjoy ours today," he said walking away to greet others.

Just then Lena's necklace slipped off her neck and into her bra. "Crap," she said under her breath. She moved around carefully to make sure the necklace stayed in place between her boobs and didn't fall out from the bottom of her dress. This would require an explanation and she didn't have a good one at the moment. She found the ladies room. Inside, there was a struggle. She won. Somehow she managed to pull out the necklace all in one piece.

After she was given the tour around the new development and had offered her fair share of "oohs" and "ahhs," Lena called her broker.

"What now?" he said.

"Well it seems I have plenty of properties and no buyers. In fact, I also seem to have buyers with no matching properties, but that's another issue for another day. I have to do an open house. How does that work exactly?" she inquired.

"You're kidding right? You've never done an open house?"

"Not that I'm aware."

"Get a couple of signs. Do an e-blast and post it on MLS."

"I can do that. Where do I get the list for the e-blast and what kind of signs?"

The broker ran down the information with her. She hung up. "Oh beautiful wise one, you can do this. Every challenge is a good one. You have more to do because you are special."

Lena did everything her broker told her to do. No one showed up at the open house.

49

The next morning Lena played with her oatmeal. She was thinking of using it for a facial. Today she would continue to work on the seller side of things, adding more properties to her shabby list of offerings. It was a whole other world. It was supposed to be more lucrative despite the increase in expenses. She was supposed to make money regardless of who brought in the buyer. So far, her list of available properties had remained stagnant.

Advertising and marketing were added to her daily repertoire and expense report. The marketing needed to be clear, aggressive, and sophisticated enough for both the seller and buyer to be impressed. Lena created online advertising, blasts to other realtors, and flyers. For commercial properties, she had to buy and install large signage.

Ordering commercial real estate signs was a first for Lena. There were rules to real estate advertising and tricks of the trade. Residential signs were simple with basic information. A photo was added for a personal touch. For commercial, signage was more complicated. She called the sign guy.

"Sign Shop," said the Sign Guy.

"I'd like to order a sign," said Lena.

"What size, what color, do you have artwork, what price?"

"I don't know."

"What's it for?"

"A building. I'm a realtor."

"Who's going to install it?"

"It gets installed?"

She had to choose between a variety of shapes and sizes depending upon the location, visibility, traffic flow, speed limit, and available space for signage. The sign guy was helpful. She bought a big sign that had to be professionally installed. When the installer asked her where she wanted the sign, she replied, "in the ground."

"I mean, what location, what angle."

"I don't know, what do normal people do?"

Lena had no idea where a sign went or how. She assumed it depended on the traffic and visibility from the street. She walked from one side of the property to the other. She drove up and down the street, looked right and left and back again. There was an art to installing these things. She took into account the speed of the vehicle, the traffic flow, the angle of the road, the angle of the sign, any traffic signage or utility poles, where the eyes might follow, on and on. Finally, she decided, "put it there."

After the sign was installed, Lena got in her car and drove up and down the street. The sign's position turned out to be the wrong spot for traffic going north. Lena quickly put several smaller signs around the property to cover her ghastly mistake and to show the client how diligent she could be while covering all the angles. When he came out to the property for a review, he was impressed. The property was littered with one big sign that had no angle and several smaller signs angled in every direction. Lena smiled. Signage cost a small fortune.

50

As the listing agent, Lena had to study and understand the property more intimately. She did market research to determine pricing, average days on the market, and what was to be expected. She ran comparables on other properties, studied what the market would allow, priced the property appropriately, listed the property with all facts and figures, marketed the property, answered all questions precisely in a timely manner, and negotiated between the client and prospect. She even staged and cleaned the property. All of it out of her realm. If things went well, she should have the contract signed, the deal closed, and the follow-up completed. Pretty straight forward stuff.

Or so it seemed. Nothing was straight forward in real estate. If the client changed his or her mind in the middle of negotiation and decided to negotiate up, Lena played bad cop. If a seller tried to circumvent both realtors to get a better rate, Lena fought for commissions. If the seller didn't disclose all the necessary information, Lena inherited problems she then had to solve. She had to be "on" at all times, able to address all issues, and ready to secure a deal or make a new one as the case may be. The landlord/owner was often demanding, and just when there was a deal, there was an issue. The owner would then blame the realtor.

Lena's phone rang. "Hi Lena, I want you to list my property for lease," said the voice on the other end.

"Hi Mel. It will be an honor and pleasure to serve you."

"I figured as much. So how much will you take in commission?"

"All of it."

"Can we negotiate?"

"No."

Lena's sellers always wanted to negotiate commissions. She hated negotiating commissions on either side. The very question made her angry. She earned every penny. The bigger the deal, the longer it took to close. The smaller the deal, the more personal issues got in the way. Lena tried to be fair with commissions. As time went on and bills kept pouring in, she got tougher and cheaper. Clients told her another realtor was waiting in the wings to take the gig if she couldn't work with them at their preferred rate. Lena had no doubt. Realtors were like starving artists. She didn't blame them because they were. They created something out of nothing despite the fact that they had so little control over anything. She did her best to make win-win situations without giving away too much. In true PR style, she spun it and made it appear as though she gave up more than she really did. She also reminded her clients that they got what they paid for and asked them what it was worth to them to get the price they wanted and the service they expected. Half the time it worked.

51

Lena continued to work both residential and commercial real estate. She could have specialized in one or the other but again, she wasn't that bright. She still didn't have a farm. To her, it was all about free enterprise, making dreams come true and praying it all worked out. In commercial, the more experienced buyers and lessees knew what they wanted, were willing to adjust, and had more realistic expectations. They were also quick to dump a deal for a better one at any time.

The new breed of commercial buyers and lessees, however, were just like residential clients. They had a specific idea of what they were looking for, wanted what they wanted, didn't care if it was feasible, frequently changed target areas, and wouldn't accept the obvious. Lena went back and forth on letters of intent followed by leases that were 30 pages long, code compliance and zoning documents, plans for build outs, time frames, and contract requirements. The process often would take up to six months with no guarantees.

When issues arose, her clients expected her to get involved in spite of the fact that it wasn't part of her job. One realtor in her office told her "do nothing and admit to nothing" because everyone reeled in and then pointed to the realtor. This was a mantra she knew first-hand. If she got too involved in a situation, she risked being oversaturated with customer service and held liable for all sorts of things. She knew. If she became under involved, she risked losing a client or a deal and was held liable anyway. She knew that too. It was all so confusing.   Her Broker often had to remind her of liability because she seemed too often to forget. She had issues. Issues upon issues. He told her if she continued to do stupid things he would have it filmed and put on YouTube.

"One more question," she asked her Broker. "What do you do when you're on the road in showings and need a biological break?"

"Keep going," he said.

"See, none of this is good for me," she whined back.

Finding time for a biological break during a series of showings was a challenge. Lena often waited for hours before she had a shot at one. Her clients, on the other hand, had no qualms about simply using someone else's bathroom at a showing and leaving a mess. She either had to clean it up or be embarrassed because everyone knew she had been there.

In a public restroom, Lena had other challenges. She had to learn how to manipulate the automatic gadgets. Sometimes it was an automatic flush delivering a whole new sensation. Sometimes it was the hand washer that had her swishing her hands back and forth to reach the perfect spot. Other times it was the hand dryer that had her dancing all around for a quick blow. The automatics came with a lot of effort.

At a bowling night hosted by her office, Lena met a few civil and nice realtors. The Spanglish sign language worked out well and all were able to communicate effectively. She really liked her new "peeps" in the office. They were professional and kind to her. In fact, they pretty much were the only people who were these days. While eating pizza and drinking beer, Lena commiserated with her colleagues. She noticed that most didn't really want to talk about work. She could certainly understand that. However, she really wanted to know if what she was going through was normal. She broached the subject.

As it turned out, everything she was going through was normal. Scary normal. It's a whole industry of frustrated people and complicated situations. As a circle of colleagues formed around her, Lena quickly learned that every client will push and demand. They expected realtors to service them by breaking the law, circumventing agreements, being available to do their bidding night and day, 7/24/365. This did not make them evil people. It just made them difficult and, bluntly put, pains in the ass. Although, there were some in fact that were on the cusp.

One of the realtors told about a recent experience he had had with a referral that lived an hour and a half away. The new client was handicapped and wanted to move into the local area. He had stringent requirements and limited resources. After much effort, the realtor found him a place to buy and a buyer to buy his existing residence. After both contracts were executed and escrow had been deposited, the client called to cancel everything immediately. The realtor was stunned.

"Why?" asked the realtor

"I'd rather not say."

"You have to say. We have executed contracts."

"I'm uncomfortable saying. It's a legal thing."

"You will be responsible for the deposit, any damages, and my commission. Let's talk it out and see what we can do."

"I don't want to."

The realtor paused and thought about this. Then he asked, "Do you have to register?"

Pause. "Yes."

Lena didn't understand so the realtor explained it. The client was a registered sex offender and had to register wherever he moved. In addition, the condo board in the new place would never approve him. Lena was grateful for the story. Things could always get worse.

In solidarity, her colleagues sympathized with her on everything. They made all sorts of noises of support that Lena appreciated. They told her to hold her ground and keep her boundaries up or her clients would run all over her. She knew this and had seen it first-hand. Lena figured this must be her right of passage. Surely there was glory on the other side. The advice to Lena was, "Do your best to give them what they want and you will make money." She daydreamed of her life falling into place if she could just grab control of it. While others talked of their experiences, Lena saw the beginning of the end. She would find patience, forgiveness, and hopefully a living at 50.

52

Another day in the office. Lena was smiling and nodding confidently at a client. It appeared they had been at it for a while. Her broker walked by after the client left.

"I see you're getting along better with the clients?"

Lena stared blankly at him. She took out earplugs.

"Sorry. I noticed within the first five minutes people say what they want me to know. After that, I don't need to listen but they still want to talk. These solve everything. Win-win."

Lena went back to her computer. The phone rang. A Russian woman with a thick accent she couldn't understand spelled out the words with associations she couldn't understand. "H like klsyoihewr, A like iweruoi." Buyers called for the same things over and over again. They expected her to do plumbing, assumed she was a therapist or at least cared, and swore a house existed when it didn't. All in varying voices: nasal, raspy, rough, so soft you couldn't hear them.

Culturally, Lena found it interesting to work with people who came to Florida from all over the world. Everyone bought Florida at some point. But it was also very confusing. Half the time she couldn't understand their preferences or accents. She changed her own speech pattern and accent, constantly trying to explain the real estate process that she herself was learning to people from the Caribbean, Latin America, China, Iran, Israel, Canada, France, Romania, Chicago, and New York.

They all had their own way of doing things with décor and negotiation. She was often confused by their customs and beliefs in how business should be done and with what kind of attitude. She had no clue what was going on most of the time.

They all wanted a slice of the American Dream. Americana. A good deal. Freedom. Security. To Lena, it was the ultimate joke. Real estate didn't offer these things. Once upon a time it did. As the country grew, land became more important. But the reality is, most people don't look at the true costs and time value of money. If the property is bought with cash, there is no mortgage and the owner doesn't have to hold insurance. But there will always be taxes, maintenance, and upgrades. If one lives in a condo or homeowners association, there are extra fees and assessments when others don't pay the fees or when upgrades and changes are made by condo commandos. Residential real estate, if one is lucky, appreciates 5% a year on average. If that money were put away into another investment, it could be much more. The main benefit is that real estate will always have value, whereas a stock can go to zero. However, real estate values can go down and one can get "under water," owing more on the property than it is worth. A rental unit to live in can be cheaper and safer in many respects. Still, most people revere real estate ownership. Image can really be everything. Even if they can't afford it, people will fight for what they think they want.

A client called.

"Lena, it's Jim. Do you know what time we are meeting?"

"3 p.m."

"Where is the place again?"

"410 SE 8th"

"Do you know how to get there?"

"Your GPS does."

They hung up. Lena's phone rang again five minutes later. It was the same man.

"Lena, it's Jim. Do you know what time we're meeting?"

"Yes.… 3 p.m.," Lena replied, very confused.

"Where is the place again?"

"410 SE 8th."

"Do you know how to get there?"

"Your GPS does."

They hung up again. Lena wasn't sure what to say so she thought it best to give the same exact answers, especially since nothing had changed. Better to keep things simple and consistent.

Another client called and said she hadn't understood that she was signing a contract. Perhaps the words on the top that said "Purchase and Sale Contract" were not clear enough. A is for apple....

A service Lena belonged to referred a couple to her as potential clients. She called the number.

Lena spoke with a man who had a voice that reminded her of Jerry Lewis.

"My name is Samir Abdul Hamim Waddah Zafar Yasin." Lena paused. "But you can call me Sam," he said. She was relieved. They discussed properties, needs and wants, and financing. Since it was an introductory call, Lena asked specific questions. It had taken her months to learn the importance of a productive screening. There really was no manual. Her real estate course didn't mention this either. Finding out a client was not prequalified or that she had the wrong criteria was an expensive waste of time. If she didn't ask, for sure the client would have no financing or means to buy anything or, worse yet, would be searching for all eternity for something that was way off the mark and didn't exist.

They agreed to a showing.

"What time are you available?" Lena asked.

"I am available anytime tomorrow," said Sam.

"Great, how about 10?"

"No, can't do 10."

"How about 2?"

"No, can't do 2."

"What time *are* you available tomorrow?" asked a frustrated Lena.

"Anytime. I don't have a car. You can pick us up," said Sam. Lena pressed the mute button and had words.

53

She began the next day by giving herself her favorite pep talk. "Good morning sunshine. How are we working towards our millions today? I love you oh so beautiful, wise, rich one. Opportunity is boundless."

Hungry, she stuffed food in her mouth while driving. In the moment, she bit her finger. The phone rang.

"Ollo," muffled Lena.

"Hi Lena, it's Mark," said the phone.

"Uh huh."

"I need help with the financing. You see my daughter...."

Listening, Lena continued to chew. After a moment, she placed the phone down on the seat next to her and let her client talk.

"Lost satellite reception," the GPS voice said.

"What? Seriously? Please find me!" a panicked Lena yelled with full mouth and food flying all over. The nightmare was beginning.

"Make a U-turn," said the electronic voice.

"Okay, good."

She noticed a sign that said "Blind Driveway." How can a driveway be blind?

"Make a U-turn."

"I just did."

"Head north 2 miles."

"Okay."

"Head south 2 miles."

The deep labor breaths started.

"You have arrived."

Lena stopped suddenly. Her car screeched. Bouncing back from the forward thrust caused a sharp pain to travel up and down her neck. She saw that she had indeed arrived. Her breathing calmed.

She got out of the car holding tea stained crumpled papers and greeted what appeared to be a Middle Eastern couple.

"Hello Sam. You got a ride, good." Lena had driven Sam Zafar Yasin around for the week. She was happy for the break. He talked incessantly and had issues with everything. He snorted mucus from the back of his throat rather loudly and often.

"Dis is my lady. Yes, my cousin."

"Nice to meet you. Where are you from?"

"Canada."

"We just came back from the Smokey Mountains. It was beautiful and very exciting," said Sam as they walked up to a quaint small one-story house.

"Really?"

Sam nodded. He snorted and commented, "Yes, very adventurous."

"Lovely."

His phone started to ring. He took the call as they walked into the house. He had several phones that continuously rang. They walked around and inspected the house.

"Looks like solid bones," said Sam

"Yes, yes solid bones," Lena agreed.

"CBS Construction."

"Yes, what you said."

"Interesting facade."

"Very."

"The neighbor said a woman died and was found five days later in the house. She was bloated from flood water," said Sam.

"Oh that's okay," Lena explained authoritatively. "When someone dies in a house they love, there will be good spirits. Anyway, this is not a flood zone. Surely that guy must want to buy this house himself. It's a steal."

"Yeah, let's buy it," Sam decided.

"What will you do with the belongings in the house?"

"We'll give them to the immigrants."

"What immigrants?" Lena pictured wayward people coming into the yard with push carts from the "old country," people arriving on boats, and others living in tenement housing.

"There is an immigrant group nearby."

"You mean American wannabees?"

"Yes, I hear they're good workers."

"Good to know. So, done and sold!"

A two-thousand dollar commission. Only fifty or sixty more to go. She cupped her hands and held them to the sky. "More please," she said to the universe in her best Oliver Twist impression. Then she went home, ate a Fuji apple, and cut her own hair.

54

Lena continued with research and showings. Paperwork flew back and forth daily. She was surprised to find so many people still used fax machines. They couldn't download, print, or scan documents. When the terms were finalized, the contract often had to be rewritten for a clear and clean copy, but who could read what the terms were? Lena had to double check every section of the contract, run back over to the client's abode, hear about their day, trials, and tribulations, smile and nod, smile and nod. In her mind's eye, she was pleasantly violent. In life, she focused on getting the signature so she could send it over again to seal the deal so that perhaps one day, two to three months from now, after she had accumulated more debt, she would get a check she would have to share with her broker. Really, it was all good. "I love and appreciate my job. Money comes effortlessly to me."

Lena reviewed everything in detail again and again with her clients. Despite her best efforts, they weren't interested in being that thorough. No sooner had Lena returned to her office than the buyer would change his or her mind about something. She would then have to run back over to where they were to make the change. For clients who were traveling, had no electronics at all, or were out of control, Lena finally had to remind them of things called business centers. Time flew by. She was aging by the minute.

On the flip side, a few of her clients were in fact very technologically savvy and she had to keep up. Lena did personal site reviews via the cell while her clients remained at home or abroad on a sofa. They also used the same system to call her live at all hours, regardless of what she was doing or wearing. It was a whole new Jetson age they didn't teach in real estate school.

As for her own technological development, Lena understood that the new and improved tools available to realtors were terrific. She could set up property videos, websites, flyers, and all kinds of marketing paraphernalia. Recently, she had learned how to text attachments on her phone. She was also looking into new kinds of directional GPS systems. It was all so exciting, for a short time.

Eventually, she learned to hate cell phones. All the connection options made her crazy. She could remember when they were coveted, not everyone had one, and they were only used for emergencies. Each call was billed separately so there were fewer calls. They were also big enough not to get lost in a purse. Now, everything was through the phone, all in one place in a place she kept losing. Lena received constant texts, calls, emails, voicemails, and more, all on one unit, all with varying noises she learned to despise. The flow of communication was further complicated with things called speaker, mute, add a caller, and blue tooth.

Once she confused the mute button with the speaker and her listener heard not only the obscenities but every other embarrassing things as well. Well, accidents happened.

She changed the ring tone to a more pleasant sound, like little fairies dancing. It made the calls from her attorney and others a bit more welcoming. She was trying out others. If she had to behave like a Pavlov dog, the experience might as well be pleasant.

55

On the home front, Lena had other technical difficulties. Aside from a GPS that kept losing her, her ten-year-old computer was not working very well. This added to her daily frustration and need for self-medication. She was always a firm believer in keeping things until they died rather than replacing them for the sake of simply being updated. This time, however, she had no choice.

She did her best to work with it. She took her computer over to her neighbor Neil's house for a refresh. He was a computer whiz. While he was looking over the computer, she perused his place. He had the same townhouse model as hers but his was neat and organized. He didn't even have little spots of clutter. Because of that, she noticed the Playboy on the living room table. She inquired about it.

"Isn't that cool," he said. "Look at it."

"Why, why would I look at it?" asked Lena, her head bobbing and arm twitching.

"It's in braille."

"Then, what's the point?"

"I guess the blind really do buy Playboy for the articles."

Neil did his best to help, but the computer didn't improve. Lena was desperate for a system she could depend on and finally gave in to charging another thing on her credit card.

She attempted to buy a new computer online and was immediately overwhelmed. "I don't have the time for this. Utterly ridiculous," she said as she looked at pages and pages of options online. Her hair was beginning to stand on end again. There were thoughts of icing. She called Susan. Susan knew everything. She ordered the model Susan suggested. It was delivered four days later.

"How do you like your new thing - the computer?" asked Susan.

"Nouns go first you know. I love it. It's the most excitement I've had all year."

"Really, that's what it takes?"

"It turns me on that much."

"Amazing how our needs change at 50."

"Now if it had artificial intelligence I'd be all set. I bought orchids."

"Really, you?"

"They're so high maintenance."

"Are you sure?"

"The ones that I have are supposed to be watered daily because they have no water system of their own. Why is everything dependent upon me?"

"That IS rather odd."

"They're like my clients. And the brothers. Sucking the life out of me."

"The brothers are completely dependent upon everyone and yet they appreciate no one. You're the strong one. Be grateful. "

"Yeah, it's not really a blessing."

56

Lena met her father at his condo, again. This time he was with her Aunt Martha. Aunt Martha was the complete opposite of her father. She was a bit bohemian, non-judgmental, talked a lot, had no problem living on air, and didn't give a hoot about finances. She got by and was well loved.

Naturally Lena cooked and served. While in the kitchenette, Martha chatted.

"I've decided to become a Buddhist this year," she said.

"Why? And why this year in particular?" Lena asked.

"I just feel like I'd like to be in the moment. You should do this; it will be healthier for you."

"What do we do?"

"You do nothing but enjoy. You meditate and live each moment as if it's the most important one."

"Interesting. I'm not sure I would like the moments I am having right now to be THE most important ones."

"This is something you should think about. I've lived so long because I concentrate on every moment and can't wait to see what happens next."

"Not sure I want to focus and remember everything."

"Focus on the future," directed her father.

"I'm also working on the Publishers' Clearing House sweepstakes. I'm down to the fifth cut. It says I will win if I make it to the end."

"I don't think I've met anyone who participated in those sweepstakes."

They continued to talk some more. After Martha left, Lena turned to her father.

"Why can't you be more like her?"

"She's high."

"What?"

"She made medical marijuana cookies for a friend who has cancer. Then she ate them."

"Marijuana Martha! Isn't she like 80?"

"That's how it starts."

Lena left shortly after her father turned the lights out on her again. On the way home, she stopped by the "Only for a Dollar Store" and picked up a new dishwashing wand, the second this quarter alone. She doesn't even wash that many dishes. Another day, another dollar.

57

Lena continued to learn that the tedious and exhausting client search for property and execution of a contract was just the first phase in making a deal happen. Once the contract was accepted and executed however, the reality set in. Clients freaked out. And so did she. Nothing prepared her for the time consuming details and effort needed for the follow-up.

Contracts came in all shapes and sizes. And then there were the riders and addendums. There were riders and addendums for condo associations, homeowners associations, short sales, any changes and updates - think it and name it, it was there. If someone breathed, there was an addendum! She made up a song using the tune from *Fiddler on the Roof's* "Tradition." "Ad-den-dums! Addendums! Ad-den-dums! Addendums!" She sang and danced around the office. No one got the joke.

The second tier of work included setting up the inspection, title work with escrow and HUDs, appraisal, the Homeowner's Association approval, plus anything else that reared its ugly head. She kept up with contract requirements, correspondence, the law, and client needs, whatever and wherever they might be. She answered every question by all parties and listened to everyone's complaints. It was important to be careful because at any given point, any one of the players involved could make or break a deal and the realtor could be held responsible. She was expected to remember everything, so she bought a memory book on CD to help her. She tried to find a "memo mate" but was told that they no longer existed. The CD said that extra stress in any form caused loss of brain neurons and forgetfulness. Continued stress would cause permanent damage. A quandary for Lena.

Once the contract had been signed, Lena moved to set up the inspection. Coordinating the inspection was an effort with a series of calls between the inspector, realtors, owners, and possibly tenants. Lena's inspector was always punctual, made time for her when she needed, and kept things moving forward. Within hours, her buyer had the requested reports. He explained to her the low down in layman's terms so she could easily recite the information to her clients. She had no clue what he was talking about most of the time but repeated it anyway. What others knew always amazed her. She replicated the same process for the appraisal.

The closing process was tedious. Lena was often confused. She didn't know where her job began and when, if ever, it ended. The title company, attorney, and bank provided added assistance. Lena liked having someone else she could send the clients to for information and personal bonding. She did whatever they told her to do. It seemed many people enjoyed telling her what to do in fact. She was happy to relinquish control. Once the closing took place, the broker took his cut. All she got was the feeling she was the star of a Charlie Brown Halloween special.

Some lenders were overwhelmed themselves and dropped the ball. At times, mortgage brokers or lenders yelled at her and bullied her to divert attention from what they were doing or not doing on behalf of the client. One of her clients overextended himself financially and the mortgage broker blamed Lena. Another client refused to accept the fact that the seller wouldn't take ten thousand dollars less though he had already taken five thousand off the price on an already low-end property. The lender wouldn't lend more and told the client the seller's reduced but not-reduced-enough price was Lena's fault. As a result, Lena lost the client. In return, she gave out the lender's phone numbers to the worst clients she knew who would waste a bulk of his time.

58

During the whole search, buy, and close process, Lena also had to deal with a variety of realtors. Some agents were just crazy. Lena believed anyone in sales had to be a little unbalanced. In order to be a great salesperson, one had to have a great threshold for pain and rejection which resulted in insanity and a rise in bipolar behavior. What made some even crazier was the sales training that promoted, "A no is a delayed yes." Denial. Fascism.

Delusions of grandeur were apparently also a big part of the job. Realtors pumped themselves up in order to offset the constant rejection. When people said they wouldn't buy or list, realtors had to continuously believe it wasn't true. Their premise was that eventually every client would buy or list. They would appreciate everything done for them. They would know the agent was the best thing that ever existed. See, delusional.

Lena tried to keep pumping. It hadn't taken off yet. And it was exhausting.

Lena worked hard at being professional and courteous to other realtors. A good realtor network behind the scenes was crucial. For the most part, realtors liked to work win-win deals quickly and move on to the next one. They could be helpful with support and guidance. Lena learned a lot about doing business this way. She discovered that negotiation, creative thinking, and finalizing the deal with others could be somewhat enjoyable.

And then there were times when Lena ran into a tough realtor. Though she met awesome professionals, she also met realtors who were shady, chauvinistic, lazy, and slimy. Sometimes their attitude wasn't their fault and had more to do with the clients they represented. They also had identity issues. It was apparent by the way they dressed. They talked at Lena about the deals they did, the money they had, how little they worked, how the Board-approved contracts were wrong, how everything Lena did was wrong, because, well, they knew best. They didn't share commissions equitably, respond appropriately and timely, or participate in a fair manner. Some tried to circumvent her. Others took to becoming a low-cost listing service for owners and investors to sell direct, cutting other realtors out of the picture. Others just simply undercut their commissions to work on volume, forcing their colleagues and associates to fight even more for business. It could be a regular pissing match.

59

Other realtors weren't the only challenging show stoppers and competition. Unlicensed "Bird Dogs" found properties for a fee and eliminated the need for a realtor altogether. Wholesaler investors bought aggressively from the off-market lists or the foreclosure markets and sold properties at lower than retail prices to investors and end users. Online services ousted realtors from large-volume market segments.

Lena knew it was tough to compete with these lines of products. She worked harder by offering personal services for the investors and owner-buyers. But when the investors competed with owner-buyers, she was torn between the two. Bank-owned properties often exasperated the problem and slowed down the process, causing realtors to lose good deals.

When dealing with foreclosures, the banks were a source of great angst. They continued to control the market, the same market they had previously destroyed. They were determined to make even more money and take their pound of flesh on all levels of the housing market. These bank-owned properties, aka REOs, which stood for "real estate owned," were no longer good deals and were becoming increasingly difficult to obtain. The banks controlled which properties got released and which would be held tight for a better offer. They decided the price, terms, and time frames. They created bidding wars and cash was king. They cut no breaks. If they honored a deal, it was incredible. For even more fun and excitement, banks quite often took the same properties off the market, put them back on, took them off, demanded unreasonable terms, then made a buyer and/or realtor do a dance just to turn everyone down flat again. Buyers, investors, and all the realtors in between were stressed to the limit. And there were a lot of addendums!

When banks gained control over properties, they either rehabbed them and sold them at standard market value with or without a tenant, or they sold them at market rate without any rehab whatsoever.

Once a bank foreclosed on a property and previous owners or tenants had to move, the bank left the property vacant until they processed what to do next. This often took a while. Sometimes the property needed repairs. Sometimes the previous owners were so angry they made sure the property needed repairs. Other times, squatters came in and added their own accents to the vacant place with urine and trash. After all, why buy the house when you can sleep there for free? Vandals joined in the fun and ripped out copper wiring, metals, and anything else they could grab to sell. Both left quite an impression on showings.

Some banks tried to find ways to work with the previous owners by allowing them to remain as tenants. In these cases, the banks sold the properties with the tenants in place, allowing investors to either benefit from an income stream or gamble on a deal that might become a problem in the near future.

As the price of bank-owned properties rose to market value and above, aggressive investors began to go elsewhere. This left an opportunity for potential owners who hadn't had a shot at properties in years. Unfortunately, the remaining properties were left in such desperate need of costly repair and rehab, the value wasn't there. So yes, potential owners had an opportunity, but only for overpriced properties that were labeled "as is," essentially unlivable. New owners who bought the property with a mortgage would ultimately become underwater with the repairs they had to make, thereby perpetuating the ugly system. Lena was thankful for the roof she had over her head and made a vow to protect it.

In speaking with her broker one day, Lena announced, "I'd like to start a Realtor's Anonymous group."

"That's an oxymoron," he replied.

"I'm overwhelmed. Not only do I have to continuously deal with clients in all shapes and sizes, I have to deal with other realtors, lawyers, lenders, title people, appraisers, inspectors, and the rest. All of them can make or break a deal or take or make blame."

"And your point is?"

"And the competition never ends between bird dogs, online services, wholesalers, and BANKS. I can't be the only one losing my mind."

"Lena, you are in the people business, the most unpredictable business there is. No matter the competition, if you do your job right, you'll make money."

"That's not true. I had three deals in a row and the banks dumped them for more money."

"So what you're telling me is that the bank is doing its job? Making money."

"Anyone can make money at the expense of others. Is that what you're telling me to do?"

"No, I'm telling you to work smarter. You know what the bank wants. More money. You need to find clients willing to work with a bank. Stay on top of the bank every minute until closing. Educate the buyer, communicate!"

There were so many responsibilities in her new job. How would she keep up? Where was the standard operating procedures manual located?

"I don't like people. And I don't like banks."

"Then what would you like to do for a living?"

The next day, Lena had to deal with a bank on another property. This made her tense again and as a result her neck bothered her more than usual. She found some topical menthol ointment in the house and applied it so she wouldn't have to walk around all day with a heating pad. A short time later, her cats became disturbed. They jumped on her and bit her neck. She ran out of the house to escape, taking her phone with her. She called Susan.

"I've been attacked."

"Oh my god, by whom?"

"The Things."

"Maybe you should have named them."

"Seriously."

"What happened?"

"I don't know. I put on some ointment and sat at my desk. I didn't disturb them at all. I was very well behaved."

"Did the ointment have menthol?"

"Yes."

"That's like catnip."

"Are you freaking kidding me?"

"I'm afraid not."

Lena threw her phone down and reached for the hose. Neighbors looked on as the wild-haired woman hosed herself down. Neil approached.

"Menthol huh?" he said.

Lena gave him a look that warranted no reply.

"Hear about the Vervet Monkeys?"

"Excuse me?"

"They're in our complex. We're not supposed to feed them."

"Well now my life's complete."

A wet, wilted Lena entered the house and continued to the bathroom. After drying off somewhat with a towel hung on her shoulders, she sat back at her computer. She dialed, and dialed, and dialed.

"Hello this is Lena Gorman and I'm a realtor. I have a client who is interested in seeing your house on Johnson. Is it still available? Great, what time is good? Thank you. I'll confirm." She hung up and dialed.

"Kim, we can see the property at 3." She hung up and dialed.

"Your tenant is not available after all? Okay, when?" She hung up and dialed.

"The tenant is not available at 3, how's 4:30 work for you? 5 is better? Okay." She hung up and dialed.

"5 is best. Great confirmed." She hung up and dialed.

"Kim, we're on for 5. See you then." She hung up.

Lena printed out information for the day's showings. She was interrupted by a knock at the door. It was Kevin.

"Hi Lena. Sorry about last night. I lost track of time and then had to run out to fix my phone. Nice tree. Look at that car."

"Kevin, you keep running late and dropping the ball. And you're in crisis mode all the time. It's too much work for me. I've got so many things going on myself."

"I know. I'm just going through a tough time. Please bear with me. Did you see that expo on bears?"

"Me too. I gotta go."

"Can we talk later?"

"Do you mind that I'm a slob?"

"Not if you don't mind me cleaning up after you." Dreamboat. "What do you have?"

"Speak to you later then."

Lena closed the door and looked at the clock. It was 11:30. She still had a full day of showings ahead.

60

Lena had been working on a short sale, another bank controlled process. Short sales were anything but short. A short sale happened prior to a foreclosure and allowed the owner to get out of the property before he or she lost the property and ruined his/her credit. Sometimes the owner even walked away with a little money and a stipend for moving. Essentially, it was a process in which the bank would approve a sale for less than the amount of the outstanding mortgage. In addition, they could still live in the property until the closing. Unfortunately, short sales were nightmares for realtors.

Lena, her client, and the other realtor did everything and anything to send paperwork to the bank in a timely manner. They re-sent it all repeatedly because it had become outdated repeatedly as the bank dragged the process out month after month. Her client was anxious. He had family visiting from out of the country. They were staying in a hotel and it was costly. Finally the deal was approved and everything was moving along. A week before closing, the property was unexpectedly sold at auction to someone else. Just like that, gone, along with the client's hopes and dreams, Lena's commission, and all the relationship building she had done with her client. Lena's client and her poor bank balance were left with nothing. So much time and effort wasted. Everyone was upset. The condo association, the owner, and even the bank representative himself had no inkling as to what had happened. One arm of the bank didn't seem to know what the other was doing.

Her client said he would never work with her again. She offered to pay some of his closing costs on another unit. He came back. She got to do the whole thing over again, now at a discount.

Lena had another short sale opportunity two months later with a new client. She found him a dream house in need of repairs. The offer went in at the asking price. After the inspection, the buyer lowered the offer as the house was in need of more repairs than anticipated and he wanted to renegotiate. Six months later, the bank responded with a price ten percent higher than the original asking price.

"Why did you go up in price?" Lena asked the bank representative.

"Since the property has been on the market for so long, values went up. The bank is correcting the price," he replied.

"How is that appropriate with so much work to be done on it?"

"The bank only cares that the values in the neighborhood went up."

"It wouldn't have gone up if you all released the property in a timely manner. You're asking for fifty thousand more than the asking price on a property that needs one hundred thousand dollars' worth of work. The seller's already signed for it."

"Doesn't matter. Does your client want it at the new price?"

Naturally, the buyer didn't want it at the new price. A month after the contract had been cancelled, the bank sold the property for fifty thousand less than the asking price, a price her buyer would have paid had he been given the opportunity.

61

Lena tried to continue to work with the banks and potential owners. She thought she found an avenue with the "first look" program, a community bank program. First time-home buyers had a limited chance to see and put in an offer on select properties 15 days before investors could bid on them. However, the banks didn't have to accept anything during this period and oftentimes did not.

There were no real rules and regulations in dealing with this program. Banks could still do whatever they wanted. Buyers who had been waiting years to own a low end property of their dreams were pushed aside for investors who had ready cash. After the allotted days passed, banks set new deadlines for offers. Once those deadline passed, they forced bidding wars for the "highest and best offer," pushing the price even higher.

Properties were also listed on open bank auction sites and all offers had to be uploaded. Everything could be viewed by the general public. Bidders held off their best offer until the end so they could see what others were doing, just like in live auctions. Then they would go for the jugular. Those who "get it" don't give it until they must. Newbies got caught up in the bidding war and bid over and beyond 2005 prices. What a racket.

Lena received a call one day from a tough commercial client who had bought from her in the past. This time he was interested in a multi-million dollar house that had been on the market for some time. It was now listed on a bank auction site as a distressed property. The buyer promised her the listing for his current multi-million dollar house when this deal was done. Naturally, he wanted to negotiate the commission. It was a win-win and her first big multi-million dollar deal. She danced around the room from twist to pony to swim.

Since the property was owned by the bank, there were the usual irregular and frustrating issues. Lena's buyer had offered the highest bid at seven million. The bank wanted another $500,000. Her buyer offered to split the difference at $250k. Since the buyer didn't match what the bank wanted, the listing agent had to contact the other bidders and offer the same opportunity to split the difference. No one matched it. Whew, she was lucky. Lena affirmed to herself, "I am the greatest realtor ever. I am a deal maker. I will make and appreciate money."

After a couple of weeks, the listing agent called Lena to finalize the deal and to tell her what she had been longing to hear. They won the bid and she would get enough commission to pay off all her debt. All she had to do was log the final bid on the website. She followed his instructions. Just as the contract was to be executed, the publicly displayed updated bid caused a ripple of interest, and a new bidder suddenly appeared with a cash deal for fifty thousand more. The bank executed the new bidder's cash offer, casting Lena's bid aside.

"Lena, this is Bob from the bank regarding your client's offer of seven point two five."

"Yes Bob, we got it?" an excited Lena asked.

"Unfortunately, no. A fourth offer came in for seven point five cash and the bank accepted it."

"What? There were no other offers at the table. We had the best one and it was accepted."

"Yes, but the bids weren't closed. Since no one offered the full asking price, the bid remained opened until negotiations closed and there was final execution of the contract. When we logged your bid as the final, another offer came in at the asking price in cash. The bank accepted it. If you can beat that price, the bank may reconsider."

"So if we had come in at the asking price before now, we would have gotten the property?"

"Yes."

"And if we offer more now, the bank may reconsider."

"Yes."

Lena hung up and stared at her computer. Finally, she dialed.

"Carl, it's Lena. Someone new came in at seven point five cash. The bank accepted it."

"How could this happen? We were the highest offer. The bank already agreed to accept it."

"Yes. Verbally. The bank didn't have a final sign off or close the bid."

"I can't go higher. That was it for me. I don't like the way this business is done. This bidding could go on forever."

"I'm sorry Carl. I'm really sorry."

Just like that, it was over. No commission, nothing. She had really needed this one. Her appliances broke down, one after the other, including the air conditioner during the South Florida summer. Her refrigerator made a pounding noise she eventually got used to.

62

One by one, no matter what Lena did, the deals still fell away and time was wasted. She was trapped by REOs, short sales, auctions, investors, clients poached by other realtors, inspections, appraisals, and financials issues, etc. She was going the wrong way, and all of it was out of her control.

Now she had a client that made offers so low they were embarrassing and doomed to fail. Lena warned against doing this, but the buyer insisted and added, "We're counting on you to fight for us."

When making one of his offers, a listing agent screamed so loud, Lena held the phone away from her ear. "Are you kidding? Your buyer isn't serious! I won't present this offer! I just won't!" Lena stood firm. "You have to, by law, present the offer." This only angered the woman more. "My seller already turned down 90 percent of the asking price!" Lena's ears hurt. She told the buyer. He insisted she continue. Two more realtors had the same reaction to her offers.

While the buyer continued his visit in Florida from Wisconsin, he had his mail sent to Lena's office. She picked it up and delivered it once a week. She was confused as to how she ended up doing this. And after all that, he bought nothing and left town. Lena put him on automatic updates and secretly hoped he used others, preferably the realtors that circumvented her along with the lender that pissed her off. She had names and numbers handy and shared them regularly with her more extreme clients.

63

Lena considered that real estate simply might be the wrong field for her. A friend once commented, "Real estate is for retirees, second incomes, and second careers." No one ever actually made it a goal or dreamed of becoming a realtor. It just wasn't one of those careers. There were 2.5 million agents/brokers in the U.S. in a career where no one needed experience or education, only a license. One could have been a failure, fired from all jobs, disbarred, etc. and still become a realtor. Lena had in fact met all of these people.

She researched the salary information on the internet and learned only too late that realtors made an average of 30k per year. While the crab her cat chased into the house clicked and scampered diagonally across the floor, Lena thought in dismay that she couldn't do average or $30k. She had to figure out how to make a living wage in South Florida, pay her debt off, and save for retirement. With the annual expenses associated with being a realtor and basic living expenses, average just wasn't going to cut it.

A realtor paid for mandatory Board fees amounting to one thousand or more a year, online subscription listing and referral services for another two thousand or more a year, and the lock boxes and Supra subscription that added at least another two hundred and fifty per year. Advertising was probably the biggest expense outside of referral fees and could take up to 30 percent of the commission. Ads or signs were purchased in full, shared, or paid per click. Most of the time, they incorporated touched up photos that looked like mug shots with a smile. Lena refused to use photo ads. The photo on her driver's license was enough intensity for the year.

Travel expenses piled up as well. They included gas, parking, and car maintenance. Lena taught herself to handle car maintenance with all the essential fluids. Home office maintenance was another story. The required continuing education and license renewals were added to the list. And at the end of it all, the broker takes his cut too. The good news was that realtors were independent contractors and could deduct these expenses, as long as they made money. Of course they had to pay their own taxes too. What about the cost of doing business that was not so tangible, such as the hours spent driving all over the ends of the earth to show a property at all hours of the day and night at the buyer's convenience? What about when the buyers were late and caused an issue with the next appointment and the rest of her life?

64

It was 5:00pm and time for Lena to meet her father again for dinner. As she knocked on the door she realized dinner with dad was the only reliable thing she had left. He didn't answer so she let herself in. Surprisingly, he was off the couch. He was dancing to the song "If I were a Rich Man" from the *Fiddler on the Roof* soundtrack. He continued as she prepared dinner. They ate at the small dinette in the kitchen as "Fiddler" remained playing in the background. Lena was glad he had finally gotten rid of the 8-track and was able to make a successful transition to a CD player.

"Money makes money," he said.

"And the money that money makes, makes more money."

"Who said that?"

"Ben Franklin."

"Ah, I taught you something useful."

"Yes, too bad about that. You know, this real estate gig is the hardest thing I've ever done. There's so much work and so many things to do. It never ends. And no one even respects a realtor. Not the client, not the lender, no one. I miss PR. At least I knew what I was doing then. I was even good and made a little money."

"Stop taking yourself so seriously."

"Okay." Step Ten.

Lena's father handed her his used paper napkins.

"Save the napkins. They're still good," he said.

He got up, walked out, and shut off the lights while Lena was still in the room.

"Really? Every time?" she said.

65

On the way home, Susan called.

"What's up?"

"Not me. I keep losing deals, money, and time. But Martha is. She's as high as kite."

"Speak."

"Well, as of a couple of weeks ago, My Aunt Martha is now a Buddhist who eats Marijuana cookies."

"Nice. A regular Marijuana Martha."

"Sounds it, right?"

"Want to?"

"Want to what?"

"Have some Marijuana, Mary Jane, MJ, Pot."

"Really?"

"Yeah, why not?"

"What do we do? How do we get it? What do we do when we get it? How much does it cost? After we smoke, do we just sit still?"

"All good questions."

"The last time I tried it, it was the 80s and I laughed for ten minutes and fell asleep for six hours. I feel like I've been in a daze ever since. But I do have little phallic pipes from a hemp fest."

"Maybe your sample wasn't good or something. It's 30 years later. Let's try the new and improved stuff."

66

Shortly after Lena and Susan planned their MJ night, Lena's air conditioning broke down. She hurriedly fixed it with a credit card. She wanted to be able to entertain appropriately. It was bad enough the place was a mess, it should be filled with summer heat too? Nope, she would clean and fix immediately so that time with Maryjane would be time well spent. There was intense pressure to get it all done before the big event. They were just days away from the soiree.

She took out her new dollar dishwashing wand and started to scrub. After five minutes it broke. The sponge head dangled. *&^&%#$E!!!

Since she was low on gas, mad as hell, and needed the exercise to get back to the zone, Lena stormed the mile to the "Only for a Dollar" store with wand in hand and sponge head dangling. Between the heat, anger, and overall frustration with life, her hair began to stand up again as she pounded the pavement. When she finally arrived, her hair was up and out and the tears in her eyes were rolling down her cheeks, South Florida sweat was running all over her body and a funky smell began oozing from her pores. With disdain, she realized she hadn't showered yet. Still, she was on a mission and needed focus. She flung open the door.

"I'd like to return this," she cried out in what sounded like a combination of a howl and a whine as she held out the broken dishwashing wand with the dangling head. All store activity came to a screeching halt with the unexpected outburst.

The young man behind the counter stood still. He looked across the store at his co-worker and motioned with his head, a signal to bring out the manager.

"Hello? I see you see me. I'm looking right at you. We're speaking the same language. Aren't we? I mean, really, aren't we?" She was confusing herself. She shook her head to clear it.

"Yes, ma'am. I'll have the manager come out," said the counter man, knowing full well if he didn't answer, things would get worse.

The manager crept up behind her.

"How can I help you?" said a man with an indescribable accent. Startled by his sudden arrival, Lena turned.

"I want to return this. It broke the first time I used it."

"There are no refunds."

"But it broke!"

"It's a dollar."

"But it's my dollar. It's hard earned and I don't have many."

"It's a dollar. Store policy says no refunds or returns."

"It's my dollar. I want a refund or store credit."

They stared each other down. Shoppers watched. Lena was not budging. The manager looked around and realized he had to do something. If he gave back the money, he might open a door to more problems. If he did nothing, the madwoman would never go away. He wanted her to go away and not return.

"Ma'am, I am sorry for the dishwashing wand. I take full responsibility. The store policy is no refunds or exchanges. However, I understand your frustration. I personally will give you the money because you are important to me as a customer."

Lena stood in silence for a moment. Skeptism turned to joy.

"Really, you would do that? Thank you, thank you," she said as new tears of happiness ran down her face. She was smiling and crying. The manager handed her the dollar. Lena took it and continued to hold out her hand.

"Tax."

He added the six percent.

"Here, here, take the wand and tell the owner to buy more quality products," she said pushing the wand with the dangling head at the manager.

"It's a dollar," he reiterated.

"It's my dollar," she said sternly, warning him to end the conversation.

"Listen, keep the wand. Maybe you can fix it at home."

"Really? Wow, okay. Thank you. You are a good man."

"Yes, yes."

"I'll be back soon."

"No need."

As soon as Lena left the store, the manager went in back and reimbursed himself the dollar and six cents. As for Lena, she left the store feeling exhausted but satisfied that her mission had been carried out successfully. She walked the victory mile home. Later that night she superglued the sponge head to the wand in an attempt to fix it and use it to clean for her upcoming gathering. The glue took hold with the wand, her fingers, and everything else in the vicinity. Somehow she finished the dishes and the whole operation was a fait accompli.

Finally, the day arrived and so did Susan. With great anticipation, the two friends sat down to light up. After a couple of tokes, they laughed about the fact that there was nothing funny. They ate whatever looked interesting and watched movies. They fell asleep on the couch. A pleasant break. Uneventful, but pleasant. Maybe they did it wrong. They would have to try this again.

67

Susan and Lena thought they needed a little fun out on the town and met at a bar for a drink. As they sat indulging in appetizers, Susan scoped out the place. Lena was agitated by everything she saw and heard.

"I think you need a, you know... one of those things," said Susan pointing. "Didn't you have one?"

"A man? Really? Because men are so wonderful? Two brothers who screwed me over followed by one who's milking me for everything I have left. And that one, the abbreviated one, he's very confusing." replied Lena.

"Seriously - a laugh, a little joy. Look around at the options."

"Okay. Here's the skinny on men. They come, they go, always the wrong men, always the wrong time. They vacillate between their alter ego and inner child. I must be a great sounding board, because they share a lot with me. In fact, they share everything but money."

"Maybe it's their age. I hear men get more sensitive as they get older."

"Cheap too. Women don't. Therein rests the predicament. We get better and more focused. I don't know where men have the time and energy to be so sensitive. They talk so much. And I'm not in the mood to really listen. On top of that, I keep forgetting what they're saying to me. I want and miss my preferred brand- the strong, silent, busy type. Where can I get one of those?"

"Let's go on a hunt."

"We can always shop for what you need on the internet. Why just the other day I met an Aborigine Jew. Where are my glasses?"

"How's work? In your cleavage."

"Thanks. Work is like men. Deals come and go and nothing sticks," Lena said, as her head bobbled.

68

The following week, Lena was called for jury duty. Ah. Another American institution. She had been waiting years for this and wondered what took so long. It was a welcomed relief and a day off. It even paid. She blocked off the day for the case and hoped she would be chosen. For once, she'd be chosen. She waited for several hours before her case was called. She was sent to another room to hurry up and wait some more. She made phone calls and used her computer. She was quite fine not doing showings. She handed everyone her card and hoped the extra effort would be helpful. She was just so happy to be in a courtroom on someone else's case.

Finally, the potential jurors were led into the courtroom for scrutiny. The case was about a man who was on parole for carrying an unlicensed weapon. He had recently been caught with a gun in his car, thereby violating his parole. The jury had to decide if he was guilty.

The judge asked if anyone felt they should be recused from jury duty. A few people raised their hands. One was a teacher at a major university in Miami. He said he should be excused as the case was in conflict with what he taught. The judge asked him what he taught. "Political science," he replied.

The next question was whether or not anyone owned a gun. About half the group raised their hands. Lena was disturbed by the ones sitting closest to her. The judge asked the hand raisers one by one what kind of gun he or she owned. One very petite woman owned seven rifles. Lena wondered how she could even hold a rifle.

Another potential juror was asked about his past.

"You've been arrested and served jail time?" asked the judge.

"Yes," replied the potential juror.

"Did you have your rights restored?" asked the judge.

"I don't know."

"Yet, you own a gun?"

"Yes."

Dismissed.

When one of the attorneys asked, "Does anyone know what presumed innocence means?" Lena excitedly raised her hands, "I know, I know." The attorney pointed to Lena. "It means you're innocent until proven guilty." The attorney agreed she was correct. Lena was delighted with herself. The attorney explained to everyone in the room the more extensive version of the definition.

Next the judge asked Lena about her sister the attorney. What did she specialize in? Lena answered, "Insurance defense," she replied confidently. Dismissed. Unbelievable. She couldn't even get hired as a juror.

69

With a heavy heart, Lena went back to her real estate work. Calls, showings, follow-ups. Calls, showings, follow-ups. The season was starting again in SoFla. Between October and May, there would be heavy traffic and more accidents, as tourists and resident tourists hit the streets.

Despite everything, Lena was still excited about the holiday season. On the big Halloween day, she laid out the candy she had prepared, selected, and been eating all week. She was eager to greet the kiddies. Last year she had run out of candy. This year, she planned ahead. She waited. And she waited. Finally, the doorbell rang. She jumped over Things 1 and 2, ran to the door, flung it open, and exclaimed, "Oooh, ahhh. What a scary costume." The small tot thanked her and left. She waited, waited, and waited. There were no others. She ate her candy and watched *Psycho* alone.

70

Lena continued to pump up at the gym. She noticed a man on the lifecycle next to her. He was reading a script. He had an auto magazine behind it. She was intrigued. She wondered if he was a producer, a writer, an actor. She leaned over to see the script more clearly. She almost fell off the machine. That wouldn't have been good.

The man seemed to have a type-A personality. She knew because he flipped the pages often and loudly. She was afraid to speak with him. His phone rang. Despite the "no cell use" sign, he had a full conversation with his mother. Everyone around him was privy to it. "Yes, ma. It's all taken care of. No need to worry. I told you, it's done."

Lena brilliantly deduced the man took care of his mother or perhaps even lived with her. She was intrigued even more. For the next several weeks, she stalked him.

She watched the gym man talking to people and working out. He appeared normal, but she had been wrong before. He had a booming voice. "I went out with this woman the other night. She wasn't pretentious. Nice person who didn't have airs," he said aloud to a man next to him. Hmm, thought Lena. Interesting.

She saw him another day speaking to the same man. She walked circles around him to eavesdrop more easily. "The guy wants to keep his rights on the project." Lena knew he was referring to the script. Now she was sure of it. He was in the biz!

Two days later, while she was on her lifecycle machine, he walked by.

"Hey," she bellowed. The man turned around. "What do you do?" she asked still on the machine.

He came over. "I'm Jack."

"Lena. Don't mean to pry. What do you do?"

"I'm a used car salesman."

"Oh, I saw you reading a script."

"That's my friend's. He likes me to read his writings and give feedback. I like to read them at the gym because I can read them easier than I can read a book when I work out."

"Ah, okay. I write a little myself."

"Really? Me too. We should hang out."

Alter ego. But nice. Appreciates the boobs. She was pumped.

71

A couple of days before Thanksgiving Lena headed over to Susan's house for their annual baking of the cranberry bread. It gave them time to talk, catch up, and drink wine. Susan was very particular about her cranberry bread recipe. It was her grandmother's, from "the old country," and she insisted on following the recipe to the "T." In years past, Lena had succeeded in following the directions exactly. She felt confident she could complete the task again accordingly, despite the fact that she had dummied down a lot over the past year and was on the verge of a nervous breakdown.

They walked into the kitchen. Lena's phone rang. She ignored it.

"Wine and white stuff," said Susan as she handed Lena a glass of wine and led her to the flour, baking soda, baking powder, salt, sugar, and other sundry items. "Finally some time just to hang."

"Yumm. Tasting it already," said Lena as she accepted the wine.

They set themselves up in the usual assembly line. All Lena had to do was prepare the white portion and hand it off to Susan. Susan blended it with her other ingredients and put it in the oven.

Watching Susan, Lena commented, "You're a hard-core perfectionist. You know, with your perfection and my sloppiness, we'd make the perfect person."

"Indeed! So, what's happening? And what's with the phone? It doesn't stop ringing."

"It doesn't and yet, absolutely nothing is happening. Have you noticed I changed the ring to be more fairy like? It's pleasant."

"Yes, very pleasant."

"People constantly call with things I can't help with or get paid for. There is way too much communication in this business. I'm an extrovert who needs a lot of quiet time."

"Better than absolute continuous silence."

"Real Estate is one hell of a business. On top of all the work, the lawsuit is also killing me – hearings, the prep work for hearings, the lack of control, the wondering how it's all going to turn out, the expense, the anger, and the bitterness. Oops, sorry Jenny," Lena said as she tripped over a dog.

As Lena and Susan moved around the kitchen, Susan's dog Jenny followed. She was often tripped over and stepped on. She was a ridiculous dog. She couldn't hear or see and was very often confused. No one really knew what to do with her or even what type of dog she was. She had to be carried up and down the stairs, to and from each room and then outside and inside when she needed to use the bathroom. And yet, she was oddly ugly adorable.

The phone rang. "Hold on, I should probably take this one," she said.

"Lena," said her attorney.

"Crap," she responded.

"They want a confidentiality agreement."

"They want a confidentiality agreement on what? We're in litigation. On something they're supposed to give me anyway? Do they know I'm the one calling the shots and they owe me?"

"They're all wrong. But it wouldn't really hurt you either way and makes us look good to the judge."

"I look harsh if I push to get my money back? Fine. If it helps the cause. I just keep giving and I don't seem to get anything back. Are they on the market yet?"

"Not yet, but they say any day now."

"Nothing has happened in the last 24 months. They just can't make a deal…. Write it up, I'll sign it, but I doubt they will."

Lena turned back to what she was doing.

"You okay?" asked Susan noticing her friend was a little more off than usual.

"I have moments. It's hard getting past things so I can move forward. Especially when my new world is much worse. I was happy, excited, elated. Then taken apart piece by piece, even getting separated from my own contacts and business. All the signs were there. I can't believe I followed them so blindly. It will take so long to recover from the damage. I'm so ashamed of what I did. And now it never seems to end. If I only had a brain."

"Are you seriously blaming yourself? These people are, you know, like, like, experts. Pros! That's it, pros. They took you and other bright awesome business people as well. The good news is that you're now at the table making deals where you should have been all along. Where are they? They can't do anything for themselves."

"Well, I guess both of us are at the table and neither one of us is making deals."

"They're frauds and will never change. There's hope for you yet. Their deals are all about the money and how much is in it for them only. Yours are all about the other person and what works for them. Neither one of you are good at creating win-wins and both of you are desperate. You just have to figure it out."

"Great."

"They can't make a deal unless it's one where everyone but them loses. As for you, you're like ego centric and yet full of low self-esteem. Gets you in trouble every time. Embrace yourself."

"I'm losing everything over this and every time I move forward with my life, something else happens."

"And by the way, there is no shame in believing in something and taking a risk for it. It's courageous. This was something you believed in and you went for it. Maybe a little extra due diligence would have helped."

As they talked, they prepared the items for baking. Lena squinted while she worked on the white stuff.

"Well, I learned my lesson. I didn't need to or want to, but I did."

"Did you ever think that maybe the lesson was for them to learn? Think of it the other way, that you stopped them for doing more damage. Why didn't you try and save your business?"

"Interesting spin. The universe has a strange sense of humor and apparently I'm the punchline. I can't imagine how this would be a lesson for them. It doesn't seem to be sinking in. I just couldn't go back."

"How do you like your Broker's...you know," Susan asked changing the subject.

"Office? Love it. None of us speaks the same language but we smile a lot, hug a lot, and have a water cooler. We talk around it in Spanglish sign."

"And the networking?"

"A living hell. The young 'uns lack listening skills and know absolutely everything about nothing. They talk at you like you're just learning things for the first time and only through them."

"Yes, good times," responded Susan.

"They want things fast and easy but deliver just the opposite. Aside from cone head haircuts, they change names and abbreviate everything. Deck and landing pages have replaced PowerPoints and websites from the early part of the century. We only ever changed names. Richard was a Dick and George was Irving. It's just how it was."

As they talked, they continued preparing for baking. Lena squinted while she worked on the white stuff. "Huh."

"What?"

"Nothing," Lena said more to herself, a little deflated.

She realized she hadn't read the recipe correctly. She had mixed up the baking soda with the baking powder. She read it without her glasses and the wine threw her off. She began to panic. She was afraid to tell Susan. It would be a horrible scene. Lena gulped her wine and poured another glass. She hid the knives. She looked at the empty glass. Hmm. That didn't help. She prayed.

"Please, please make sure this bread comes out okay and tastes right. Help me, help me, help me." Lena made the sign of the Jewish star on her chest. She turned to Susan. "Alright it looks like I'm ready."

"Great, let's throw it all into the oven," Susan said.

"And out to the universe!" Lena replied as she threw her arms out to embrace air.

Lena continued to pray nothing would happen and that the bread would taste the same. Though they've been friends for years, Lena knew that Susan could be rigid in her ways. She would certainly flip out. Lena said nothing. Forty five minutes later the bread was rising and rising. It looked a little green.

Frowning, Susan asked with charade arms flailing, "Did you, did you follow the recipe?"

"Yep," replied Lena avoiding all eye contact with Susan.

"Exactly?"

"Of course," she lied.

"I wonder why it's rising like that. It's falling over the sides of the pan."

"I can't imagine why. We'll just have to wait and see how it tastes," assured Lena.

"Something's wrong. It's got a green tint. Maybe it's the... the machine."

"The oven? Really?"

Susan reached in the drawer and pulled out the manual. Lena drank more wine with her back to her friend. She continued to clean the counter, something she never did at home. She stepped over Jenny as she moved around the kitchen. She was getting buzzed.

Lena put up her hand up and waved. Then she left her arm up and bent her hand at the wrist and moved it side to side. Susan looked up from her manual.

"What are you doing?" asked Susan.

"I'm inventing a new wave," replied Lena.

"I can't figure anything out today."

They talked some more and checked on the bread again.

"This looks about done. Let's taste it," said Susan

"Yes, let's."

They took the bread out of the oven and put it on the counter. They cut and tasted it.

"Not bad," Lena said impressed and surprised.

"Actually, quite good. How weird. I'll have to wrap it differently this year to account for the new shape. Other than that it's pretty good. It's just so strange."

"Oh, it happens to me all the time. Sometimes things come out differently than we expect but just as good. You just never really know what's going to come out of my oven. Especially when it's on fire."

The mystery remained unsolved.

72

Christmas and Chanukah were just around the corner. Lena had to prepare. She was broke and concerned. For some, misshaped cranberry bread
just wasn't enough. She perused the house to see what could be re-gifted
or recycled into a new wrapped gift. She had plenty of unopened bottles
of alcohol. Lots of people gave her alcohol. She didn't know why. She also
had promotional makeup packages and almost new purses. Wrapped up,
those would do. She found a nice supply and selection of bows, cards, and
wrapping paper from years past. Yep, she was armed and prepared.

The phone rang. Squinting at the Caller ID, she answered.

"Hi. It's me. Want to go shopping?" asked her sister.

"No, I don't really have the money or anything to return and I don't
need anything," Lena replied.

"Shopping isn't about need. It's about greed," said the well-fixed and
well-paid attorney sister. Nice.

Lena thought a moment. "I guess I do need some workout clothes
since leotards and leg warmers are out. I have some gift certificates around
here somewhere I can use."

Really it was about need. Though her closets were overflowing with
clothes she hoped to someday wear again as well as those she had to give
away before she lost her mind with clutter, she was in desperate need of
workout clothes. Clothes she actually intended to wear now, in the "zone".

"Tomorrow at 5 then."

When Lena's older sister wanted to go shopping, it was mostly for her-self. She liked holiday shopping and specials simply for the sport. Lena knew her sister had the right attitude. Shopping should be an experience one could enjoy. For the most part, Lena hated shopping to begin with and more so now that her funds were limited. The holidays were worse. Her shopping choices these days had dwindled down to pretty much what she could afford and needed, mostly food. She could have two apples, or one apple and half a banana. In addition, her growing hatred of people, coupled with her even lowered tolerance for bad behavior, added to her lack of funds, made the prospect a nightmare.

73

From the moment she walked in the door, it was as bad as she expected. A worn out woman said, "Welcome to Smartmart" in a very dull voice that only resulted in making Lena feel extremely unwelcomed. People called her "Mrs." or "Madam," and she didn't know why. Others walked by with phones attached to their heads.

Then there was the attire and overall presentation. Another missing manual? Really?

The dress code was crazy. How could people walk around the way they did? Did they look in the mirror before they left the house? Was it really anything goes in the store? Shouldn't the décor and humans be representative of what was available? Was this actually what was available? G-string panty lines outside of the pants were not good looks. And then there were the spandex challenged. Clothes were so tight they were almost transparent. Other wearables were so loose there was no point. A woman walked by practically naked with a mask on her face. It made no sense. And the gum! My, oh my. Chewing like a cow was never attractive. The cracking was obnoxious and infuriating.

Lena asked a young man (she could say that because she was 50) where the sports section of the store resided. He looked out in the distance. She repeated herself. "Excuse me, Excuse me. Where is the sports section?" He kept looking ahead. "Hello, Hello?" She followed his stare and looked ahead, seeing nothing unusual. She spoke more loudly. He just stood there. Finally, she walked away and shook her head. "Weird. Just plain weird." Maybe he was insane. As she passed a variety of things she longed to buy, her heart sank and her head continued to bobble.

Lena wanted service, compliments, and validation. In the old days, customers came first. They were catered to. They were complimented and made to feel good. They were always right. These days, Lena had to wait to be acknowledged even when she was the only one in the store. Service was out of the question. Every point had to be argued while she continued to be insulted.

"I service people day and night for very low pay and I expect the same in return. It's included in the price of the item I'm purchasing. Now I'm just a lost old lady that shakes her head amongst people who are half dressed talking to air."

"Calm down, it's the holidays," her sister reproached.

People continued to walk by with phones attached to their head speaking aloud to no one. They had personal conversations out loud with themselves for everyone to hear and not appreciate. They were alien creatures in lines, among the rows of clothes, and in the bathroom attached to the mother ship.

"Why do people worry about privacy on the internet and at the airport when they walk around half dressed, totally exposed, and connected at the most inappropriate times? People practically invite you into their private lives with everything they say and do," said Lena.

Lena was not interested in hearing about hemorrhoid surgery, family dysfunction, credit information, what was for dinner, and how much weight someone gained. She also didn't care about what the boyfriend said to his second girlfriend, what lipstick was best, anyone's work woes, and the affair that was so apparent. This constant connectivity was insane.

Everything was so "out there," and not only with cyber cells and clothes. A couple walked by arguing out loud. Someone sneezed next to her without covering his mouth. Another walked by with curlers in her hair, while someone else walked around in pajamas.

Then there was the "bump." No matter where Lena was in the store, people ran into her, with never an "excuse me." She made such a point to stay out of the way and maneuver into an area where there was little or no traffic. They seemed drawn to her like magnets yet refused to acknowledge her presence. Even as she entered the store she got bumped. When she walked through a parking lot that was 90 percent empty and saw no one else around her, she got bumped. She got bumped out of nowhere, even when there weren't any distractions involved. How was this possible? Did people just not see her? Why was she such an idiot magnet? Maybe it was because American traffic went right and everyone else went their own way. Nothing seems to flow anymore.

"Everyone keeps running into me."

"Act like you're deranged or poor and they'll leave you alone."

"Well, I kind of am at the moment," she said bobbing her head and twitching.

74

Lena eventually found the section she was looking for. What a selection! Such an array of colors and styles. A buffet for the eyes! Choices! She wanted the yoga styled sleek pants and top. New workout shoes too. She was told she should get rid of her sneakers every six months. She had used hers for over a year. Oh the joy!

But the moment didn't last. The checkout was frightening.

In line, Lena was shocked and appalled when the man next to her let out a huge yawn without turning his head or covering his mouth. Not only could she see his tonsils and every filling, she could also feel and smell his breath. She wondered what disease she had just contracted. A simple touch of modesty was always appreciated, yet rarely used.

"God, kill me now," she said to Lori.

They continued to observe.

"Do you think people share their life stories and problems and various kinds of intimate and personal information with the woman at the check-out, or is it just with realtors?" Lena asked Lori.

"The line moves too quickly," replied Lori.

"Not this one."

"We're almost done. Focus on the pretty nails."

"Long and colorful."

"She can't manipulate the register so efficiently."

"I don't think she's in the efficiency business."

Lena acknowledged long and colorful nails on the woman at the register. It was hard not to. They seemed to get in the way and were distracting. She stared at the nails. She was amazed by their beauty however annoying they were. Some of it was actual artwork. She assumed all of it was expensive. Lena admired those who took time out of their busy schedule and allocate the funds for designer nails so they could work at a discount store. Then she could stand in line while they took forever to manipulate the gold or diamond studded nails over the keyboard of the cash register. Lena herself could barely sit still long enough to get through a simple paint job, and she chronically smudged. She wondered what the nails would be like on a chalk board or, better yet, how they would feel being pulled off one by one in a Middle Eastern torture chamber. My how her mind could wander!

"Look, her stretch pants are ripping. I didn't know they could do that," commented Lori.

"The fun never stops."

After some time, Lena bought one outfit and a pair of shoes, all on sale with gift certificates.

Despite the grueling experience, she was so in awe of her purchases that she didn't touch them for weeks. They were perfectly placed with their price tags under her Christmas tree and menorah to be admired and appreciated with pride and excitement. They sat revered right next to the unopened scarf box given to her by the Prince of Monaco until well after the holidays.

75

Lena was back in her home office when her phone began to ring. She picked it up.

"Hi Lena," said her attorney.

"Crap," replied Lena.

"I haven't said anything yet!"

"You will."

"They haven't honored their settlement. What do you want to do?"

"Kill them."

"I didn't hear that."

"I didn't say that. It's tough. The debt is overwhelming. I'm doing everything I can to start over and move ahead. It needs to end." Lena frantically looked around muttering to herself, "Crap, where's that file?"

"I know. I'll motion for the judgment."

76

Trying to stay in the holiday spirit, Lena attended a networking function and sat down next to what appeared to be a pleasant woman. The woman, ne Kristy, had just moved to SoFla from the Midwest. She was a young, recent retiree. Her voice was whiny and she had a smoker's hack. They exchanged cards. A few days later, Kristy called.

"Hi Lena" she hacked. "It's Kristy, we met the other day."

"Yes, hi Kristy, how are you?"

"Doing well, thank you." Hack. "I'd like to buy some houses to flip, around the 200k price range. I'll also need a place for myself, something decent in a nice neighborhood around 400k."

"Great, what's your time frame?"

"As soon as possible."

"I'll work on it right now."

Bonuses for Lena!

Lena researched properties while Kristy stayed in a hotel. After Lena selected properties she made a list that was then discussed, analyzed, visited, and reviewed.

First Kristy wanted to flip lower end properties. After several weeks, she decided she wanted the higher end flip because there would be less competition and possibly more money. Lena did the research, on command

and on demand. She ran all the investment numbers, comparables, and neighborhood research to find a deal that would make Kristy happy. She set up several showings. After extensive research and a series of showings on 38 properties, Kristy decided she wanted to go lower end after all.

Lena pushed a button on the phone and had words.

"Lena, Lena is that you?" asked Kristy.

"Sorry, wrong button. Someone else entirely. My pleasure to serve."

Lena went back to her computer, switched her focus back to lower-end properties, and began the process all over again. At the same time, she continued to look for an appropriate place for Kristy to live.

The phone rang. She placed it on speaker and continued her work on the computer.

"Lena speaking, all about me, how can I make it all about you?"

"Lena it's Dad."

"You don't sound like Dad."

"Cut it out. It's about Dad. He's fallen."

"And he can't get up? Hello? Sorry. What's happened?"

"We don't know yet. We're at the doctor's."

"I'll be right there."

Twenty minutes later, Lena entered the doctor's office with a sick feeling. She joined Lori and George in the extra chair in front of the doctor's desk. Films hung on light boxes.

"It's a benign brain tumor. It's blocking some hearing and obviously causing balance issues. It's been there too long. It has to be removed as soon as possible," said Dr. Miloff.

"Oh my God. Dad, didn't you feel anything?" asked Lori.

"I just thought he wasn't listening to me," commented Lena.

"The surgery is an intricate one. There are only three specialists that can handle it. The closest is in New York," said the doctor.

"What can we expect?" asked Lena.

"Paralysis, stroke symptoms, or possibly nothing. There's always a slight chance of expiring in, during, or just after surgery as well. You should be prepared and have your affairs in order."

"Oh my god, oh my god, oh my god," responded Lori.

"Okay, okay, Dad you okay?" asked Lena.

"Yes, I'm fine. Let's go."

Later that evening when Lena came home she threw her mail on the table. It flew across the table and landed on the floor. There was a knock on the door. She opened it. It was Susan.

"You're knocking now?" asked Lena surprised.

"Here" she said handing Lena an envelope.

"What's this?"

"Your ticket to New York. I know you're broke and you would never ask."

Lena paused and couldn't speak while she digested the unexpected act of kindness. It had been so long since she was the recipient of one. With tears in her eyes she embraced her friend.

"He'll be fine." Susan said as they pulled apart.

"I know he will be. He's the most resilient person I know. We have nothing in common. I'll pay you back as soon as I can."

"It's my holiday gift. Just accept it."

"Come in, let's wine."

77

Going through airport security check was an enormous affair. Lena felt pressured for time even though she knew she would be sitting for another 45 minutes. She could feel the people behind her and it stressed her out. Her scarf and jacket went into the bin, shoes and bag, into the bin, computer out of the carry-on, into the bin, toiletries, into the bin and the carry-on itself straight onto the rollers. Finally, her shoes. She worried if her socks had holes or were clean. She forgot to check. Once the security check was finished, she put everything back together in reverse. It was a lot of effort and angst.

While waiting for the plane, the three busied themselves. Lori took out a stack of papers and highlighted things. George read the *Wall Street Journal*. Lena said her affirmations. When the Hari Krishna's came by the girls huddled next to their father so as not to be noticed. He shrugged them off. Lena's phone rang. It was Kevin.

"I wish I could be there. Tilapia," he said.

"I know. You just can't. Another issue. Are you grocery shopping?"

"Yes. I'm there in spirit."

"So are my ancestors." They chatted briefly and hung up.

The phone rang again. It was Kristy.

"Hi Lena, it's Kristy. I'll take that unit 612 if you can make it a lease to own."

"It's listed for sale. I'll see what I can do. You never know."

Lena paced as she made calls while waiting to board the plane. After some back and forth on the phone between the listing agent and Kristy, she was able to negotiate a lease with an option to buy to her client's advantage. They were able to lock in the price and hold the property until Kristy committed to the buy. Kristy was comfortable and satisfied. All was fine.

On the plane, Lena endured an assortment of smells and sounds. It was hard to relax. Every time she dosed off, the stewards woke her to ask if she wanted something to eat or drink. Now annoyed and awake, she wondered why people who babbled the most had the worst hearing. She waited until her bladder was going to explode before disturbing others to use the bathroom. Just as she sat down in the bathroom, turbulence began and the seatbelt lights blinked on. The pilot cautioned all to return to their seats. Lena had a hard time concentrating on the agenda at hand and held tightly to the ADA compliant handrail. She was not leaving until she finished. She couldn't stop anyway. She tried to think of something else hoping it would speed up the process.

At baggage claim after landing, the trio passed an old lady singing "Beat it" by Michael Jackson. She had some spunk that one.

On the way from the airport they took a shuttle to the subway, transferred to another train, and walked three blocks to the hotel. She passed an eclectic array of Wall Street skyscrapers, a myriad of architectural wonders, creative masterpieces, along with a variety of neon, sexy-girl, and midget wrestling signs. There really was no place like New York.

Despite her miserable mood, Lena appreciated it all. She was entertained every step of the way. The subway was the best. Someone yelled out his plight and begged for money. A man talked intimately to his own reflection in the mirror and kissed it. She wondered what kind of affirmations he had going on. Outside, street singers and dancers provided even more entertainment.

When she got off the train, Lena looked on as people mulled about, seemingly going nowhere. Someone stepped on her foot. She thought she might collapse from the pain.

As they headed to the hotel Kristy called again.

After more extensive research on lower-end properties, Kristy decided she now wanted to buy wholesale properties and changed her search again. She received a list from a wholesaler and wanted Lena to review it.

"I'll send you a list someone sent me. You can review, run comps and tell me your thoughts," Kristy hacked.

In order to avoid issues down the road, Lena explained that wholesale prices did not include realtor fees as they were, well, wholesale. "No problem. Just remember that I'll need to add my fee onto the cost. The list you have doesn't include realtor commissions."

"I don't know why I need to be responsible for realtor fees."

"That's the case when the seller isn't compensating the realtor and in this case the sellers aren't. I don't work for free. Maybe you can deal with them directly and do your own research. Sincerely, THAT won't offend me."

Lena had researched properties for months now for Kristy, working holidays, nights, and weekends. She was tired. She hadn't had one contract come to fruition and it appeared there was nothing on the horizon. Still Kristy insisted she really wanted to buy and flip and Lena would benefit.

"I don't think you should be paid on the front and the back end of a deal. Since you will get the listing anyway, why can't you just throw in all the research and work on the front end?"

"Because if I work both ends, I should be paid for both ends," replied Lena.

"If you brought a property in from your own sources and the commission was built in, then that would be acceptable, but payment on wholesale properties that I send to you is not fair."

"You're asking me to work on them and there are no guarantees," Lena explained as politely as she could muster. "As attractive as it sounds and no matter how much I want to, I simply can't afford to support other people's businesses and growth at this point in time." She added, "I understand you are under no obligation to work with me and I want you to feel free and comfortable to deal with the wholesalers directly." Lena even offered some names of others Kristy might want to work with who might also be helpful, namely the realtors and lenders who were mean and had circumvented her.

"Perhaps I could work with you on the MLS properties only. In fact," she said, "I could just get my own license and do my deals myself," Kristy added with a hack.

"Absolutely you should. With your license you can run the information yourself."

"How about a flat fee?"

"Why don't you send me an email with what you have in mind?"

"Okay."

Then Lena hung up the phone and had words.

But Kristy continued to use her. They never discussed wholesale properties again. For Lena, this was the beginning of the end. She found from experience that that typically was the case when people demanded free work.

Then Lena's attorney called.

"What now?"

"The judge ordered mediation."

"Because he sees they may be able to work a deal?"

"In two weeks."

78

In the hospital room, George was hooked up and prepped for surgery. An orderly was just finishing a review of the vitals. Lena and Lori sat by the bed.

"Are you scared," asked Lena.

"Who wouldn't be? But… whatever is God's will is what will be."

"We'll be here."

"Well, I hope so for your sake. And if I stay here, I'm with you. If I go there, I'm with your mother. Either way, I'm good and will be well cared for."

Lena wondered what made him feel so confident. She stayed with him until he fell asleep and the orderly wheeled him away.

There was nothing more Lena and Lori could do for their father at the moment, so they stepped outside for a walk to clear their heads. Lori began talking so quickly that Lena couldn't figure out the topic. All she knew was that they were supposed to go somewhere and quickly. Apparently, Lena was supposed to sign something before the end of the day. It was 3 p.m. now. They hopped on the subway, took another train, came up a flight of stairs, and then ran half way down the street. Suddenly Lori stopped, cried, and babbled incoherently. Lena was perplexed.

A homeless woman nearby came over and stood close to them. She became more intimately involved by making a threesome pact with their bodies. Lena looked at the homeless woman and at her sister and back again.

She turned to the woman and said, "Can I help you?"

The woman replied, "She's upset."

"That's evident."

"Why is she upset?" asked the woman.

"I'm trying to figure that out myself," responded Lena.

Then Lena turned back to the woman, "Still, it's really none of your business. Thanks anyway," she said as she guided Lori away from the stranger and into a drug store. They walked up to the pharmacy counter.

"I'd like some Sudafed please." She turned to Lori, who was now looking at her strangely. "Make that three boxes," she amended.

"We can only supply one at a time with your driver's license," said the pharmacist.

"Really? Okay, one for me, one for her." Lena rummaged through her purse for her license and did the same with Lori's bag. She showed both to the pharmacist.

"What are you using it for?"

"Allergies. Can't you see her eyes and running nose? Disgusting actually. And me, mine are just starting, see?" Lena pulled at her eyes.

The pharmacist was skeptical but handed the two boxes to Lena anyway. She grabbed Lori and pulled her out of the store.

"What are you doing?" Lori asked.

"Giving you midlife happy pills."

"What?"

"Take two and call me in the morning."

Lena handed Lori two pills. "Ahh!!!" Lori continued to cry.

"Oh god, how long do these things take?" Lena asked of the Heavens.

79

Eventually happy and focused, the two returned to the hospital. Their father was still in the operating room. They waited in a variety of different positions, watching television, napping, reading, pacing. Finally the doctor came out and shared the news.

The operation was a success. Lena's father was in recovery. Only time would show the effects. For now, the tumor had been removed in its entirety and systems seemed to be working properly. Lena and Lori waited eagerly by their father's bedside for him to awaken. They were grateful.

George was on a ventilator, monitors attached all around. Lori stood over her father. She studied him.

"He looks utterly ridiculous," she said.

"What is wrong with you?" asked Lena.

After a moment of observation, Lori sat down and went through legal paperwork as quickly as possible. Then she got up and compulsively moved everything around in circles. Lena was terrified she would knock out the wires that connected her father. Then her sister wanted to smoke but didn't want to go outside. In order to avoid an explosion if she remained in the room with an open oxygen tank, Lori went into the bathroom. Lena and her father were alone for the first time since being told of the tumor. She sat staring at him. Silence filled her head, machine noise filled the room, and sadness filled her heart. A few minutes later, Lori reentered the room.

"You know it happened to him too," said Lori.

"What happened to whom?" asked Lena.

"Dad. He was in a similar situation in his early 50s."

"What are you talking about?"

"Dad was ripped off by people he worked with too."

"I can't imagine that."

"He sold his practice and joined up with a team of doctors as his first step toward retirement. After his two-year contract ran out, they continued to use him and his investment. The only problem was when it came time to compensate him as a partner, they didn't. Then they claimed he didn't bill enough. Since his contract had run out they didn't see any need to even keep him on or acknowledge his status."

"What did he do?"

"I helped him sue. They were still using his resources and name and working with him as if he were a partner. In addition, you can't actually "fire" a doctor and take away his livelihood like that. And there was no document to claim he was anything but a partner. Dad worked hard with the team like any partner would and, he was too ethical to pass patients from doctor to doctor. We won."

"I had no idea. What did you win?"

"He won the suit and some compensation but he lost some of his pension. Sometimes when you win, you lose. The hardest part was that he was suddenly unemployed and unemployable. He wasn't ready to retire and he was forced into it."

"If only he had had some control."

"Control is a state of mind."

"So are arrogance and greed. Where was I when this happened?"

"In college."

Lena and Lori sat in silence.

"Why did you do it?" Lori asked.

"Do what?"

"Get so involved, give them everything."

"I thought it would be my exit strategy. I'd make a lot of money quickly, retire." She shrugged. "Share with others. I guess I was arrogant in my belief."

"An American Greed statistic with a touch of ego."

"You mean me?" Lena asked quietly.

"Yeah, you just jumped right in."

"American greed going the other way, interesting."

"Why didn't you stay in or rebuild your business? You started a whole new career which is so much harder. In one of the hardest field imaginable."

"I couldn't go back. Nothing was left. It took 20 years to build what I was so ready to disregard and have destroyed in months. I lost my referral base, clients, and momentum. I lost my confidence, my drive. My heart. Starting over in the same business would have been too painful. And what if I failed? They told me I was worthless, and without my money I believed them. Everything they said."

"Just like Jonestown."

"Saw the movie, everyone dies at the end."

They stood silently, staring at their father.

"Lena, I hate to mention this, but we have a problem with the insurance. It doesn't cover home healthcare, and we're going to need it for a while."

"Is that what was making you so crazy? Nothing else, right?"

"I don't know. Could be. I was trying to fix it but it didn't work. I think I would have been crazy anyway. He drives me insane, but oddly he's also the anchor of my life."

"Does it cover a stay in a facility?"

"For 30 days. After that, it's up to us."

"You have any money?"

"No. In fact, I owe money. I spend money as soon as I get it. I can't help it."

Lena dropped her head while the news sank in. What now? Lori took her cigarettes into the bathroom. She stopped and turned to Lena.

"You didn't lose everything. You still have a name, experience, and people. You're just not loyal to yourself. Use your imagination. And pills! These pills really work. Great focus."

Lena turned to her father and studied all the wires, his face, his hands. She folded one of her hands around one of his.

"You know, you really are the man I aspire to be as a woman."

The phone rang. She didn't answer. She was thinking how her father was the only person she knew who folded Glad sandwich bags the way they were designed to be closed. She couldn't imagine what the world would be like without him or what might happen next. He was her law and order.

80

Sometime later, Lena headed to the waiting room to stretch her legs and grab a cup of coffee. She returned her calls. The first one was to Kristy.

"Lena, I need to move earlier."

"They already told us no several times. There's a tenant and a contract."

"It's a conspiracy! What am I going to do?" Lena pulled the phone away from her ear as Kristy hacked into it. "I have two dogs and things in storage that have to move! I'm going to cancel the contract."

"You don't have anything else right now," explained Lena.

Lena's first instinct was to find her a place or even offer up her own. She would have to clean of course. She slapped herself to snap back to reality. It was not her problem. The move-in date was always clear. Kristy claimed there were six other units available in the same complex she could move into immediately. Changing to another unit would mean Lena had to stop what she was doing, breach a contract, and sign, seal and deliver another deal, plus make everything convenient and smooth for Kristy within the next 24 hours. Kristy would be penalized and she just couldn't do it.

"You have a legal binding contract and you were aware of all the dates. If you break it, they will sue you. You also don't want to anger the association especially since you want to live there for good at some point."

"They'll take my side!"

They hung up. Lena had words. She stayed outside the room and paced as hours passed. Finally, she sat down and pulled out her computer. Pictures of her townhouse appeared on the screen as she ran estimates on sale prices and comparables on it.

81

Upon her return to Florida, Lena once again came face-to-face with her dual nemesis, this time in mediation. Their attorney began the conversation with the usual tirade - she was nothing until they met her, she had attached herself to them, and she was a gold digger. Her attorney stuck to the facts – she had loaned them money, given the brothers everything, and has not been paid a dime. The mediation was finished within an hour. No deal was made.

The following week, Lena's own FOR SALE sign hung outside her townhouse. People came in and out. They meandered about looking through Lena's things and around her house as she had done herself to others many times. Susan stood by Lena inside and off to the side stage left as she did at the Prince of Monaco's reception. They watched and waited.

"The house looks great, clean," said Susan.

"Yeah, it's kind of nice this way," agreed Lena.

"The price is low Lena."

"It has to sell quickly."

Pregnant pause.

"What are you going to do with your things?"

"Sell and donate them. I can't afford storage, and I - I couldn't afford to give my annual donations, so it's good for everyone." Lena's voiced cracked and tears began to form.

"I'm so sorry Lena."

"If I believed in something different, this would have gone another way. But it could be worse. I could have to pay someone else's commission. It's all good, really. I can pay back bills, help my father, and pay you back."

"I told you, the ticket was a gift. That's what friends are for."

Tears ran down Lena's face.

Two weeks later, a SOLD placard had been placed on top of Lena's FOR SALE sign. Lena carried a box outside and slid it into the trunk of her car. She looked back. The door stood open. Tears were in her eyes. She walked around the car towards the house and stopped. She began to shake. The tears began to flow in earnest. She appeared physically in pain. She sat on the curb and cried with full body motion, letting the last two years of pain slide out. She cried, alone, on the curb, next to the beat-up car, with the house and open door in the background.

82

Lena called Kevin and got his voicemail. She hung up and sat down next to her father. He was now back in his condo sleeping soundly at home. Lori also sat by the bed reading papers. The cats were uncharacteristically subdued and asleep on the floor near the foot of the bed. Food was on the night table.

George began waking up and was groggy.

"Welcome home sunshine. I hope you don't mind that I've moved in," said Lena.

"There are worse things."

"Really, I never thought of it that way."

"Why aren't you married?"

"I'm trying to stop the gene pool."

She read somewhere that seven generations were needed to rid the family of dysfunction.

"You're so competent."

"That's new. Hungry, thirsty?"

"Yes please."

The girls tried to keep the conversation lively while struggling to behave as though everything were normal. George put in his dentures to prepare for feeding time. Lori monitored as Lena brought the food over and sat down to feed her father. She placed a bent straw into his juice for easy access, then scooped the shredded beef and brought it to his mouth. She scooped another mouthful just as George's teeth fell out and on to the dish. There was a "splat." The girls looked down at the plate that now sported a full set of dentures in the middle of the shredded beef. Their father had lost so much weight they no longer fit. Lena and her sister stopped and stared. Silence descended.

"I think," Lena started, "you're supposed to bring the food *to* your mouth." There was a pause, and then the sisters began to giggle. They looked at each other and then at their father. He frowned. The giggle turned into a laugh. Though they knew it was cruel, the laughing was a relief. It was so quick and natural. They just couldn't hold it in. The moment was a pure one, full of the intensity of love. They had reconnected in a new way. Things were going to be okay. Though he acted annoyed, her father and his one open eye held a twinkle. The other remained droopy.

Later in the evening as Lori slept in a chair, Lena tucked in her father.

"Life is terminal." he said.

Lena opened her mouth as if to say something.

"I - I forgot what I was going to say."

"That's how it starts. Should we be friends?"

"What for? No. You're my father. You have to stay that way."

Before he could respond, he dozed off.

"But what you really are is a prince Dad. Really and truly," she said softly as she tightened the covers around him and kissed his cheek.

It took George another couple of days to focus. Almost immediately he seemed to be his cranky old self. He hadn't always been a peach but at least he was tolerable. Understandably now he was purely miserable and achy after the ordeal. As time passed, it appeared he had lost hearing in one ear and vision in one of his eyes. One side of his face was a bit palsied. His anger and annoyance brought back some of his vigor, but everyone knew he would never be the same. Lena spent as much time as she could with him. She was full of love for her father, however unattractive he was at the moment.

"You know what I'm most proud of?" he asked her one night as she straightened his covers.

"Me?"

"My 20 years as a volunteer usher at Tanglewood."

"Really? That's what you're most proud of? Doesn't really say much about you or your life does it?

As her father recuperated, Lena contemplated the family unit. It seemed like the whole purpose of the unit was for these few precious moments that stretch your heart so far to include pain on one end and joy on the other. Or maybe it was just one more learning curve from the universe.

83

When it came time to exchange payments for the deposit and first and last months' rent, Kristy didn't like the way it was being handled. She gave Lena a piece of her mind. She screamed into the phone. Lena didn't understand. Kristy emailed, texted, and screamed that she would report Lena to the Board of Realtors, to her broker, and to her attorney. Feeling threatened up and down and all around, Lena quit on the spot. She was upset and shaken and had to get back to her father.

Lena called the listing agent on Kristy's behalf to tell him she was no longer working on Kristy's account. He insisted that she come to the turnover and finish it up. Lena knew she was obligated to be appropriate and professional. It wasn't really a problem to show up. She didn't know what to do with herself anyway.

When she arrived, everyone was there, including the previous tenant. He was moving out the last of his items. The husband and wife owners were also there. The place was a mess. No cleaning or proper walk through had been done. The other agent was clearly embarrassed. "Perfect, just perfect," Lena thought, bracing herself for the explosion she knew was coming. She had no clue what to do or how bad it would get. It couldn't have happened with a worse client.

Kristy looked around quietly and stated the obvious. "This place isn't clean." The calm before the storm.

The other agent quickly responded. "We can have it cleaned. We can also adjust your rent for the inconvenience. Do you want to stay in the place while we do this?"

"I have nowhere else to go, two car loads of stuff, one in storage that has to be out in an hour, and two dogs."

The wife explained in a strong southern twang, "The tenant just moved out an hour ago."

They all looked around. Dust on all the surfaces showed clear markings where the former tenant's personal items lived. The bathroom had hair in the tub. The toilet was filthy. The furniture was worn and dirty. Used sheets were still on the bed. There were crumbs on the counter and unwashed dishes in the sink. The other agent asked the owners their thoughts. The husband looked around and exclaimed, "Looks clean to me." Even Lena's inner slob thought this was disturbing.

"The carpet has stains everywhere," commented Kristy growing irritated.

The husband stepped on a carpet stain. "What stains?" he asked.

Kristy looked around slowly. She said, "The baseboard in the bathroom is sticking out. No maintenance check has been done."

The husband walked into the bathroom. He kicked in the baseboard and called out "Fixed!" He then added, "You know you're buying a used condo. It's been used." He seemed to be dismissing the fact that Kristy was a tenant first and she was under no obligation to buy.

The other agent spoke to the wife about the dirty carpets and stains. The wife turned to Kristy and asked "Do you have a vacuum cleaner in your car? You can get it and we'll have the tenant vacuum now." No one said a word.

The owners then proceeded to share their problems with Kristy. The tenant had been there for two years. He asked to stay an extra day. They allowed it because he was a friend. They had just arrived an hour ago after driving five hours from north Florida. They were confused. They didn't want to be landlords. They really wanted to sell the unit. They were elderly, lived far away, needed the money, and were not interested in all these extra complications. They were doing everything they could to accommodate Kristy, as was everyone else.

"It's disgusting to move into someone else's dirty place," Kristy told Lena.   However, after some hesitation and careful conversation, Kristy accepted the place. She agreed to have it cleaned herself and to collect reimbursements for the time, inconvenience, and costs.

Next the husband and wife began to discuss furniture and personal items they needed and wanted. The discussion agitated Kristy even further. She had no furniture. The owners agreed to take only personal items and leave the furniture. Kristy had no issues with that except that it should have been done already. The owners claimed they didn't know ahead of time that they were allowed to take anything.

The owners continued to complain they had no room in the car, no boxes, and didn't know what to take. Kristy not only had no interest, she was surprised the couple was showing such lack of concern for her. Didn't they understand that she had to stay in a dirty place they neglected because she had no other place to go and that that was the priority? While she stood there exasperated, the owners remained confused. Lena was speechless.

"Are you sure you don't want that?" asked the wife.

"I don't care if you want to take that. I just need the furniture and basics," replied Kristy.

"Okay, I'll take the floor lamp and drapes."

"That's not personal, those are basics."

Finally, Kristy had enough. She would rent the place but not take possession until it was cleaned and properly prepared.

Lena suspected none of this was going to work no matter what happened. It was doomed and, yet, a little amusing. The pills must be working.

The owners remained baffled for the next hour and conversed a lot with the air. They were concerned only about fitting items into their car. They made no arrangements for cleaning carpets or maintenance. The other agent took control and arranged for a cleaning service to arrive on Monday morning. Then he left a message for maintenance to fix any issues with the condo.

Lena looked out at the view to digest everything and think about what she should do to assist. She saw an elderly man staring down three sizable iguanas. He threw out things that might be edible for them. They stared back at him. The man was one with the iguanas.

It was Saturday. Kristy left not knowing where she was going. By this time she was hysterical. Rightfully so, thought Lena. It was a quick turnover but not impossible. Timing was always a factor and caused tension during moves. The trick was to be flexible and to have as few loopy people involved as possible. On top of that, Kristy had an added burden of two animals and a tight storage move. Everything in one day just wasn't going to happen. More issues and learning for Lena. Everyone had issues, and somehow the realtors had to continuously find a way to resolve them. She was at a loss.

Miraculously, Kristy found a hotel that accepted pets. The owner credited 10 days to offset the costs. The listing agent cleaned the place to perfection. Kristy moved in. All seemed to be working out. Lena called Kristy to touch base. Kristy told her she was okay. She needed a bit of a break to get settled before starting again on her real estate investments. What joy.

84

With her father back home and needing care, Lena was doing her best to keep up. In between, she continued to receive calls from her attorney.

"Hi Lena."

"Crap."

"Again with the crap? They want to make a deal."

"I already did, four times. When will this end?"

"They want an extra 90 days. They'll give you all the collateral in advance. They claim they are in the middle of deals and want to make you whole."

"Collateral in stock that may or may not be worth anything and deals that are never made."

"You pretty much have nothing either way judging from the looks of how they do business and honor deals. However, if they give you the collateral now, you'll have an unsecured debt. The main difference is if you go for the judgment, you can collect more easily on a secured debt."

"Far be it for me to ruin anyone else's hopes and dreams despite the fact they would have no qualms about doing it to me. In fact, they already have."

"True."

Lena was torn by what-ifs. When would this end? She quickly tallied the lists of pros and cons. She didn't want to destroy anyone's visions and company, especially if she wasn't sure she would benefit. On the other hand, a judgment didn't destroy everything. It just made it harder for them and easier for her. All of it was miserable. Lena heard a loud bang and thought that was a sign from the universe.

"I really want to believe it will come to fruition, especially if I have a lot to gain, but I can't put myself at risk anymore. Clearly they are setting me up again. Let's finish this."

"It's your life Lena, welcome back to it."

"Yeah, well, it's not much better." She hung up, closed her eyes, and meditated.

Moments later, water started to ooze all over her father's Pergo flooring. It was coming from the water heater. She didn't know what to do. She became frantic. She ran around and into the hall and up and down the stairwell. "What do I do? What do I do?" she asked a silent universe. Up and down, up and down. She dialed her sister. No answer. She dialed Susan. No answer. She even dialed her broker. No answer. She ran down the hall and knocked on her neighbor's door. He told her to shut off the main.

"Where's the main?"

"In front of the condo, to the side of the closet."

"Oh."

"Then call the plumber."

"Do you suggest anyone in particular?"

"A good one."

Lena did as she was told. Then she spent the next three hours using every towel, sheet, and even clothing to soak up the water. Her father slept through the whole thing. She took pictures before and after. She was exhausted. When the plumber came, she was calm, cool, and collected. When the insurance adjuster came, she no longer cared. When the check came weeks later, she was elated and felt she had earned every penny. Her father rested and watched the news.

She now had to replace the floor. She searched online for flooring and quickly became overwhelmed. The neighbor told her to go with porcelain, so she did. She went back to the store six times until she narrowed it down to four choices. She bought samples of all and walked all over them to see how they felt. She moved them all over the floor to see how they looked in the day and evening. She called a contractor she had met through work and he gave her a reasonable quote. Together, the contractor, the neighbor, and Lena all picked the final choice. Lena and the contractor moved around her father's things, including his bed with him still in it. Lori stopped by with groceries. The floor was finished within three days.

She did it. She had dealt with another situation. Something was accomplished to her benefit. The price of the floor was less than the insurance check by two thousand dollars. She applied the money to her father's healthcare bills. For the moment, Lena was satisfied. It was a good feeling.

85

Then Kristy called. Again and again, followed by a slew of emails and a series of texts.

"The refrigerator is on the fritz and the washing machine ate my clothes," Kristy frantically bellowed into the phone.

"Things happen. Give the landlords a call and see what they say," replied Lena.

"The refrigerator is 10 years old," Kristy complained. Lena didn't understand what the problem was since the refrigerator she had had in her townhouse was 20 years old. It had had a leak and made a disturbing banging noise. Other than that, it still worked fine.

The weekend continued to go from bad to worse. There was a series of more manic calls, emails, and texts from Kristy. Lena was with her father. She called the other realtor and her broker. Both said it was a tenant-landlord issue and to stay out of it. Lena couldn't cope with the drama and had other priorities. She texted Kristy to let her know she was busy and would call later. She had no control over anything.

Lena waited it out. She saw through a string of email correspondence that the landlords and tenant were working things out after all. The landlords let Kristy out of the lease, and they agreed on the financials. Unfortunately, they expected Lena to give up her commission. The other realtor already agreed to give up his.

Lena's broker said there was no reason to give up her commission. Either way, it was up to her. He would back any decision. She had done her job and everything she was supposed to do. However, he added, if there were to be a lawsuit over any of this, it wasn't worth getting involved. Lena thought about it. She agreed with her broker. She simply didn't trust Kristy to behave appropriately and couldn't stomach another lawsuit. She gave back the commission, though she desperately needed the money. She washed her hands of the whole thing, including her client. Some deals just couldn't be made, and some cost more than they're worth.

86

Things for the close-out seemed to be moving forward, when Lena received an email from Kristy. Kristy felt Lena should have been more involved and shouldn't have disappeared after receiving her commission check. Lena emailed back saying that Kristy had told her she was settling in and needed space. All of these problems after her move in were unexpected and had nothing to do with her or her job as a realtor. She had no right to demand extra time and service that was not required. The constant calls, emails, and texts full of demanding and manic messages were inappropriate, especially when she had told Kristy that she was busy and would get back later in the day. Nothing was a dire emergency and everything could have been worked out, including the cancellation. Lena suggested that maybe Kristy should concentrate on being more grateful for getting out of this situation without being sued or owing anything. In fact, she made out quite well, having scored free weeks of accommodations.

In between conversations, Lena found out that Kristy had actually moved in earlier than she let on, even before the cleaning was finished. So she had had plenty of time for a walk through. Both the washing machine and freezer were in working order and in use by the other realtor when she took possession of the unit. Lena felt Kristy had done everything she could to break the agreement from the moment she signed it. For some reason, she had a hard time committing to the unit and the terms.

Further, nothing was ever her fault or good enough. Kristy emailed back. Lena refused to read the email or respond. In her mind, it was over.

Lena knew this was not really the best way to handle things. She was also painfully aware of the fact that she was taking months of frustration out on Kristy. She was ashamed and felt a more professional realtor would have been able to control her client. In addition, she wasn't totally sure she was in the right. Still, Kristy deserved a virtual, if not verbal, slap just for being so annoying.

But alas, the saga didn't end there. There was close-out drama. Despite all that had been done for her and the fact she had already rented another unit, Kristy was still unhappy. When she, the other realtor, and the owner arrived for a final close-out walk through, Kristy refused to turn over the unit. She didn't like the way the checks were written to her. She originally had given personal checks and now wanted and felt entitled to monies in a certified format. Seventy-five percent was in a certified check format, and the other 25 percent was a broker's check, which was good as gold. Kristy refused it.

As a last resort, Kristy agreed to sign the check over to the owner with the caveat that the 70- something woman return with cash within two hours. As it was the weekend, the owner had to go to several ATMs to cash out two thousand dollars. Lena had no clue why anyone would do that. Still, everyone wanted Kristy to move on and leave them alone, and they were doing their best to make that happen and get rid of her.

Finally, it was done and still there was a problem. This time, no one knew the reason. The other realtor called the association manager as well as the police. Kristy was forced to turn over possession of the unit. As she was being removed, she claimed the realtors were rude to her. She would file complaints. Lena was thankful she was not there. She would for sure have become violent.

87

It was definitely time for a break. Lena's favorite people now were the Macedonians and Lu. She decided to get them together for an evening of multi-cultural fun. Lu's family owned and ran a very authentic Chinese restaurant among other things. Lena invited the Macedonians to have a family dinner at the restaurant.

Lu and Lena set things up at the table. While doing so, they harmonized and danced to Motown music. The Macedonians filed in. Lena led the introductions. After some socializing, they all sat down. Light chit chat ensued. Food started to be served, one dish right after the other. None of the Macedonians really knew much about authentic Chinese cuisine, and seemed warily open to learning. Though Lu shared the name of the dishes, she was vague about what was in, on top, and around them.

The Macedonians studied the food skeptically. There was a lot of gooey stuff and unidentifiable meats, or whatever. Seven out of eight of them couldn't bring themselves to eat it. Fortunately there was one adventurous participant who ate everything. "It's good, it's good," said the big burly man with a name Lena couldn't pronounce. Her mouth just didn't go that way. The conversation remained entertaining. The Macedonians continued to be represented by the eighth man. Lu and her family didn't seem to notice.

One of the Macedonians brought a bottle of Rakjia and passed it around. Lu and her family didn't drink. She told Lena that most Chinese don't drink alcohol as they couldn't handle it well due to genetics. So, the Macedonians drank while the Chinese ate.

After a while, things got livelier. One of the Macedonians played music on his IPod. The Macedonians got up out of their chairs and started to dance traditional dances around the restaurant. The Chinese family joined in, quickly learning the three-step combo. The Chino-Mac meet-and-greet continued until the wee hours of the morning. The evening was a success. They bonded. Lena smiled.

88

Later that week, after a closing, Lena sat patiently in the waiting room of a title company with her client Fred. Fred was the seller and both were waiting for their checks. They greeted each other and sat down. Fred had a deep, loud voice from years of smoking.

"So, you married? Dating someone, gay?" he boomed.

"Excuse me?" asked Lena.

"Well, I figured an attractive woman like yourself has someone, and if not I'd like to fill that hole."

"I have a boyfriend who lives about two hours away that I see on the weekends. I also have cats."

"Yeah, all single women have cats. If you get lonely during the week, just remember I'm here."

"Well, thanks."

"You look gay. Are you sure you're not gay?"

"I'm pretty sure, but I get that a lot. How do I look gay?"

"It's your short hair. All gay women wear their hair like that. You should grow it longer."

"I can't. It just doesn't do well. And I'm 50."

"I haven't had sex in like five years and I get a hard-on three times a day."

"I'm sorry to hear that. Really sorry I heard it."

"I can tell you because you're my realtor and you have to keep things confidential."

"But you don't have to."

"I mean I love my girlfriend but she's gained like 60 pounds and you have no idea what it's like to plug that thing. We tried two and a half years ago but it didn't work out so well."

"Maybe she's just not up to it or feels unattractive."

"I don't know. What makes it even worse is that she has this daughter who's smoking hot. Makes life so difficult. We don't even like each other, but she lives in the house. With me being as frustrated as I am, it's a nightmare."

"Well maybe we can find someone for you. Hooker?"

"Na, I want someone clean. I like you because you have an elegance about you."

"Thank you."

Lena was relieved when the title rep finally came to distribute checks. Everyone left the office. Walking out, she looked down. "Well, I guess boobs are where they should be after all," she said.

89

Lena had met more people in the past year than she had in the last five years of running her PR business. She dealt with people from Section-8 clients to multi-millionaires, from highly intelligent and healthy to challenged in all sorts of ways.

Everyone needed a home, a place to do business, and a friend. They all had concerns and some form of business sense she found intriguing and quite often weird. Personalities were across the spectrum - mean, nice, needy, and devious. Each could be tedious in his or her own way. Lena tried to be objective. She tried not to hate them. She was just tired of OPP, other people's problems. Still, she was building something. She couldn't define it yet, but she was beginning to feel some kind of momentum. She wondered if she would have the virtuous patience to see it through.

90

Lena entered her father's condo. She listened to the blaring television and got caught up on the news as she entered. There he was, her father, sitting on the couch in yesterday's clothes and scotch in hand. He shut off the television and rose to meet her.

"You're late," he said blocking her further entry. Lena's father was a bit more ornery these days.

"It's just past 5:30. I was farming."

"Good to be on time."

"The later you arrive, the shorter the meeting. Although I live here now."

"The early bird gets the worm."

Her father proceeded to tell her the ingredients in the kitchen she could use for the dinner she was expected to prepare.

"Lori brought broccoli, chicken, salad fixings, and chocolate cake."

"Mind if I come in?"

George moved aside and Lena continued. George quieted and Lena moved around the abode.

"Let me know when it's ready," he said.

"Thanks for all you do," she said.

Lena cooked and served the dinner. They ate quietly in the kitchenette. Despite the 78-degree condo, Lena felt a chill. Looked like her own thermostat was off. She noticed a big supply of Irish Spring soap on the counter.

"Why do you have enough soap to last past your lifetime?"

"It's good to be prepared."

Lena sighed. "I'm tired of my clients."

"Who cares?"

"Really? That's the best you got?"

"You have clients. That's good."

"Everything is so personal and labor intensive. I feel like I don't belong."

"All business is personal."

"That goes against everything I know about business. I can't save the world, I'm busy. I'm only in it for the money."

"How's that working for you?"

"I'll have to revisit my business model." Step Eleven.

They continued to eat. George finished, got up, folded his paper napkin, and put it back in the napkin holder. Lena loved her father with his horrible etiquette, weird habits, and amazing pearls of wisdom. He took his plate to the sink and left, turning off the light as he went. Lena sat alone eating in the dark. Routine was a good thing.

91

Another lead came in from the referral service. This one was from a young man, Ian, eager to purchase a property. He had no experience with multi-family properties. Everything was new to him. After only four outings, he fell in love with a small condo building. There was a sign that said "Slow Children" on the corner. Why do they advertise this?

The buyer and seller signed the contract. The seller agreed to fix anything found in the inspection that needed repair. An inspector inspected and provided his best assessment of the property. Lena provided the seller with the repair list. According to the other agent, the seller agreed again he would fix what was on the repair list. His realtor confirmed this over and over again for the next several weeks. All was moving along smoothly.

When Lena brought her buyer in for a final site review, the repairs had not been done as specified and agreed upon. The few things that had been fixed had not been done properly. Lena's client was furious. She confronted the listing agent and he argued. Then he became abusive. In addition, he started to communicate directly with her client and then complained and yelled to her about him.

Realtor Tom said, "Your client doesn't know what he's doing. He keeps saying we have to fix everything. We have to fix basic things, not things like the light bulbs. I'm not going to deal with him anymore."

Lena replied, "Exactly why are you talking to him in the first place? It's not your place to talk to my client. You asked for his rundown and he gave it to you. You and your client had time to respond and you never did."

"We will fix what's in the contract."

"That's exactly right. You haven't done that. You are supposed to fulfill the contract and fix things with a licensed contractor. Perhaps you should read it before you start quoting it," said Lena.

The situation deteriorated. Her client said if the seller wouldn't fix the property as agreed then the alternative was to take repair credits of 1.5 percent off the purchase price, as stated in the contract. She relayed the information to the other agent. He emailed back immediately with a simple and concise "No." This told Lena that the other agent never presented the alternative to the seller and it angered her further.

"No, this is not going to happen. There are acceptable repairs and unacceptable repairs," explained Tom. He was standing by his argument, whatever the heck it was.

"Nothing is specified there. We have nothing that says what will or will not be fixed from you or your client, and we are abiding by the terms of the contract. You were supposed to respond within five days if you disagreed with anything. You didn't do that. Your client is in breach," replied Lena.

Tom continued, "I'm just telling you it's not going to happen. Your client doesn't know what he's doing and he's pulling codes that have no place here."

"I'm not going to argue with you. I'm telling you there is nothing in the contract that precludes having any of the repairs done. Not only does the contract call for repairs to be done, your client agreed to it wholeheartedly. The contract also states that they must be done by a licensed contractor. Have you seen the work? It's horrible. Finally, it doesn't matter whether or not you like the code issue, your client needs to abide by the executed contract as well as his own handwritten notes specifically agreeing to repairs," Lena replied angrily.

"Your client put light bulbs on the list. That shouldn't be on the list. My client has been a lawyer for 30 years."

"Then he should know the law. We're not really talking about light bulbs, we're talking about repairs, and if you don't do them, you have to give a credit for what they are worth. It's not up to you to decide. I suggest you and your client familiarize yourselves with the real estate law."

They argued for quite a while. Lena calmed herself and, surprisingly and oddly, the other realtor as well. They got off the phone amicably. But he called her again and again. She was too busy to pick up the phone. He continued to call, like a child. Idiot.

It was only a few days until the closing and more arguing ensued. Nothing was fixed. Lena and the other agent argued every hour on the hour. Lena was furious that this was taking up so much of her time and that yet another contract was being broken. The other agent became manic and kept dialing her number. She didn't answer because he was so abusive. So, he contacted her broker. Her broker called her. The realtor was out of control. She was not budging because she knew she was in the right. She was also drawing the line on how she would allow herself and her client to be treated. In the beginning, she just wanted to get the deal done. Now, it was about what was right in terms of the deal, what her client wanted, and how people should be treated. This time it was personal.

The other agent continued to insult her client, her intelligence, her professionalism, and everything else he could. She caught him in constant lies and misrepresentations. The unnecessary bullying was driving her crazy. She made up her mind to file a complaint.

The haranguing continued through until the day before the closing. Lena and her client held their ground. The other realtor started to unravel even more. He got the seller to give up a small amount of money. He demanded that Lena step up as he himself would do. He wanted her to contribute a $600 match from his end. She refused. Why should she pay anything? She had done everything right. The seller was not honoring the contract.

"Why would you ever think I would give up money to help your client break the law?" she asked.

"I'm just trying to make the deal happen."

"Then try a win-win. Have your attorney client abide by the contract and my client will pay according to the contract. Your attitude is "why do a good deal when you can beat someone up with a bad one."

92

The night before the closing, two of the condo owners in the same development wanted to meet with Lena and her client. She and her client went over to the site. They drank lots of wine and told lots of stories about the seller. A good deal of interesting information was exchanged. Lena drank too much wine.

The next day at the closing, Lena presented the case and went over the terms of the contract. She stuck to her notes as she didn't want to forget anything. She was shaky and uncomfortable. She was at the table and wasn't leaving until she made a deal.

The group at the table consisted of Lena, Ian, Tom, the seller, and the closing agent. The seller had glasses with one arm missing.

"Do you all have a copy of the contract?" Lena asked. The buyer, the listing agent, the closing agent, and the seller all nodded yes. "Okay, under Section 9, after an inspection is done and a list is turned over to seller, he must fix the appropriate items. In the seller's own handwriting he reiterates that he will do so under paragraph P and again in Section 12. He initialed and signed the contract. The seller had five days to object to anything on the repair list submitted and he did not object to anything. So, gentlemen, you didn't abide by the terms or your own comments that you yourself wrote into the contract. In addition, you were selling the place fully rented but you're missing a tenant which is a loss and devalues the place. How do you wish to compensate my client?"

"I don't," said the seller.

"So, you're breaching the contract?"

"No, you would be breaching if you don't sign. I've been an attorney for 30 years."

"Until you were disbarred. I looked it up. You need to step up."

The seller got up and sulked out of the room. Lena turned to Tom in shock.

"Are you kidding? What the hell?"

"He thinks you're victimizing him. You should have used a softer tone."

"Really? I spent the last two weeks being bullied by you representing him and now when presented with the facts, I should be soft, cuddly and, and personal?"

"It would help."

Hours passed. Tom read his phone.

"The seller is willing to give two thousand. I'll give another thousand. Why don't you, Lena, give another?"

"You want me to give even more? No. And I find it inappropriate to ask me in front of my client. Your client is still fully liable for the deal and my commission if he breaches the contract."

Another hour passed. Finally Lena's client had had enough. "You know what. That's fine. Lena you keep your commission. Tom, you give up your thousand, and we'll make the deal. This way the seller can get a new pair of glasses." There was a small laugh.

Moments later they signed documents.

"Are you happy?" Lena asked her client as they left.

"I am satisfied. The seller is a prick," Ian responded. "You looked like you were going to cry," he added.

"I have a hangover," said Lena. She couldn't believe she just said that. Her client laughed.

Despite the giggles, Lena was still livid with the other realtor. She wanted to file a complaint but she couldn't shake a bad feeling about it.

She spoke to her broker. He told her to make sure she was covered before taking any action. She chose to call Tom's broker and issue a warning. The realtor at least, needed a slap across the head.

The next day, the closing agent made a point to call and tell her that he was impressed. "Nice job. I'll definitely refer others. I like that you care enough to fight for the client and especially the fact that you do your homework." Awesome! She was like the new realty police.

93

After quite some time, Kevin and Lena had a moment to catch up. They sat in a restaurant making chit chat. It was apparent they were running out of things to say. The moment was a painful one.

"I'm sorry I haven't been a good boyfriend Lena."

"I know not everything is your fault. It's just how the cards are dealt. We'll always be friends "

"I wish it were different."

"I wish everything were different," said a resigned Lena.

Lena wondered if this was it for her love life. Here she was at 50 and all she had was a lot of frustration and responsibility. There was little joy and she didn't know where to go to get it. She'd keep up with her affirmations and work-outs in the zone. If the universe could just give her a sign, she'd feel a lot better.

94

Lena seemed to be learning something from everyone, whether she wanted to or not and whether she liked them or not. She shared with her journal and her psychic this journey of gratitude, patience, people, personal reflection, belief in oneself, the greater good, and solid old American values. Images of American greats such as Ben Franklin, Warren Buffet, and Bill Gates continuously ran through her head. She felt the course changing. Her credit card company sent her a letter. They increased her credit line. Then they sent a second letter offering her bonuses for her usage. Then they sent a third letter telling her the credit line was being increased even higher than it had been before this whole mess started. She hung all three letters in the makeshift office in her father's condo. Now she knew things were moving forward. She clicked on her affirmations, hugged her cats, and repeated, "I am a money magnet."

At the end of the year, she tallied up her commissions. Her hard work had actually paid off. She had pulled in almost a six figure income, well above average. She also had closings scheduled for the coming year and would start the year with money on the books and confidence in her heart. She could even speak a little Chinese, Spanish, and New York.

She was especially excited by unexpected personal referrals and repeat clients. She was building a business and a reputation. Buyers with prequalification letters researched their own properties and brought them to her for review. She finally found the file she had lost a year ago and was able to reconnect with the client, and he still wanted to work with her. One of her other clients insisted that she list his shopping center and threw in a trip to the Bahamas as a bonus. Well, if she must, she must.

The new realtor for the commercial building she purchased closed on a qualified tenant. Lena brought in the other one. It turned out that if she and her partner decided to sell the property now, they would double their money. The universe was working! It was really working! She danced with the Macedonians. Life was getting better and she was moving forward.

Despite the thrill of all things American and hope springing eternal, Lena still needed to find a way to replace her retirement fund and do all the things she loved with friends and family. Her attorney continued calling, the bills kept rolling in, and she had no guarantee of a steady income or real stability. And she lived at home with her father. She remained concerned and hoped it wasn't a permanent thing, her future reality. While thinking, she played solitaire absentmindedly on the computer. Then she went on her computer listings and continued to play. For the hell of it, she threw out an offer on a bank-owned property. Judging from what she knew, it was a good deal, but she wasn't paying too much attention and didn't take it seriously. Her online listing dabbling was more or less another version of solitaire.

95

A few days later, Lena received a call from a local community college representative, Steve, asking her to teach a class on entrepreneurship to adult business owners sponsored by a bank.

She burst out laughing. "Warren Buffet's Rule #1: Don't lose money. Rule #2: Don't forget rule number one. I didn't follow the rules. What could I possibly share with others? Does it pay?" she asked.

"You could look at it that way or you could look at it as though the best person to learn form is the one who's had ups and downs, not the one who's never struggled. Yes, there's money."

The college had a prestigious ranking. She was pleased to be asked and more so to be paid to teach compliments of a bank.

"Okay, I'm in. Being around colleges and books makes me feel smart and a bit sexy."

"Do you know a good lawyer?" the rep asked.

In the classroom, and to her surprise, she found she had a lot to say to local entrepreneurs after all. "Deals are about people. You have to know who the players are at the table. If you know the people, you know how to play the game and whether or not it's worth playing. Being at the table is not enough."

She introduced responsive recitations.

"Everyone now," she instructed. "In the words of the great Kenny Rodgers! You have to know when to hold 'em,"

"Know when to show 'em," the class responded.

"Know when to walk away,"

"Know when to run."

"You never count your money when you're sitting at the table."

"There'll be time enough for counting when the dealing's done."

"Well done. And Ben Franklin?"

"Money makes money and the money that money makes, makes more money."

It was quite an animated discussion. After the first class, the course continued with-one on-one mentoring. It all went smoothly and was surprisingly enjoyable. A few days after it ended, Lena received a call from Steve.

"Guess what?" he asked.

"Oh no."

"You were a hit. You scored the highest rating with the class. They want you back."

"Wow."

"In fact, three of the students want you to be a regular consultant with their business."

"Put a poster up, I'm wanted!"

"And by the way, Kevin was a good find for legal. He babbles a lot but he knows his stuff. Thanks!"

96

Lena thought that maybe she could capitalize with a new niche combining her experience in marketing and real estate. She didn't know if it would work, but it was a possibility. After all, what other realtor had 20 years of marketing experience? She could work for other firms or developers and make a go of it. She could market funeral plots and burial real estate along with the life celebrations business she and Susan started. She threw it all out to the universe. As luck would have it, an attorney reached out to her for work. She couldn't seem to get away from attorneys. This one represented a developer who wanted to build a large complex in her own neighborhood. The attorney arranged for Lena to be part of the team to work on community consensus building. It was a tough job and required door-to-door sales. It utilized all of Lena's skills, combining her new real estate world with her old marketing guru expertise. Piece of cake. Cake. Icing. Focus!

Lena came up against some heavy opponents. She prepared herself against those who complained about traffic and others who wanted their own new architectural designs to be adopted by the developer. Others expected bribery, or "donations," in exchange for their support for the project. Lena played the game but refused to do anything unethical. She was surprised at how easily the strategies came to her. It made her a bit crazy and unable to sleep at night because she became so hyper, but that was okay. She couldn't resist the intellectual stimulation that didn't require any popping of pills or copious amounts of caffeine.

The City, of course, had other plans. Response to the project was mixed. The members on the commission who were against the development were ruthless. They canceled meetings and actually placed a moratorium on all building in order to stall things until after the election. As a result, things like new windows, home improvements, and commercial improvements all came to an immediate halt. Lena had never heard of such a thing, especially in a tight economy where things were getting tighter. Now she had to fight the City to remove the moratorium before she could do anything else.

She could play hardball too. She knew the City was making a fool of itself. She was going for the gold. She brought supporters whose businesses were affected by the moratorium. She brought out low-income housing representatives as well as already approved high-end developers. She had 400 signatures on a petition in less than a week. She released negative publicity on the absurd action. She brought a comprehensive line-up of community and business speakers to the commission meeting. She even brought her wheelchair-bound client as a concerned citizen to speak on the dangers of delaying the installation of handicap amenities and upgrades. The City should be ashamed of itself for being so selfish, careless and reckless. Shame, shame, shame! She could say the same for herself for pulling that stunt, but be that as it may…. She would worry about shaming herself later; right now she had a mission. The moratorium was lifted rather quickly, and development resumed. Lena was building quite a reputation, but she wasn't finished yet. Now she had to win the final vote.

One afternoon, as her eyes were struggling to stay focused from a late night of community consensus building, Lena opened an email she wasn't expecting. She had won a bid on a bank-owned property. What? At first she didn't know what she was looking at and couldn't remember any offer she had pending with a bank. Then it became clear. It was the absent-minded offer she put in a few weeks ago. She won the bid for a single family home. It wasn't in a cookie cutter neighborhood, and it was now hers if she wanted it and could get a loan. She called up one of her favorite loan officers and within 24 hours she was qualified. She was qualified. Qualified! Who would have thought? She was buying a house from a bank and was qualified for a loan! Only in America.

Meanwhile her schedule for the development was tight as she visited each and every community forum and homeowners' association meeting. She still didn't like most people, and difficult condo commandos were the worst. She pushed ahead and answered every question appropriately and respectfully. She showed the development in all its glory. She wrote emails and notes to everyone she knew and encountered. She listened to people and responded. She bombarded the City with letters from very well respected players in all sorts of supporting industries. She touched on all the hot topics - energy, economic development, traffic to other area businesses, usage of public transportation, and the enhanced image the upgrades would afford the City. She sat at many tables and addressed all issues. She made a point to find the pressure points and pushed them. She still kept losing her glasses in her hair so she got a second pair. Finally, the vote passed unanimously in her favor. Lena was satisfied, excited, a little ashamed, and exhausted. When could she do this again?

97

A few days later, Lena awoke in bed, still at her father's place, and noticed that her hair wasn't as unruly as usual, and she herself wasn't such a mess. She made her tea and entered her makeshift office. It had a little order to it. She opened her email with a little less disdain and a lot more eagerness. She was met with gratitude and congratulations for a job well done. She felt good. She was slowing rebuilding her life.

It had been a tough few years. She was beginning to let go of the past and find focus in her future. She could even smile from time to time. She had no idea where the journey would take her, but she was willing to go along for the ride. She would leave it up to the universe and maintain her focus. Step Twelve. She continued to look for new opportunities and was happy that her ability to make money in real estate was opening up so many other doors. "Who knows," she said to herself, "maybe this is the job that will take me into retirement after all."

98

Back at the office Lena was rummaging through her purse. She looked up, paused, and asked a colleague next to her who couldn't understand what she was saying, "So, how many times have you had a party in your head and no one's there but you?" The woman nodded and smiled back.

Then her phone rang. She squinted at it and answered.

"What now?" she asked her attorney.

"What, no crap?" he responded.

"You've been elevated," she said.

"Doing the happy dance, which is what you should be doing."

"Why?"

"You won."

"What did I win? It's been so long."

"A million dollar judgment. Slow and steady wins the race."

"Does it matter how you race?"

"No. But if you do it right, you can win much bigger," her proud attorney noted.

"I guess the trick is to win more than you lose."

"And sometimes when you win, you lose. In this case, it's a mixed bag."

"Story of my life. What happens now? Where's the money? I'd like to know what that smells like. I have a house I need to finance."

"According to them, there is none. We're in the process of seizing their assets and receivership."

"What assets?"

"Since they claimed over and over again they have no money and nothing else, you can grab the patents and the stock."

"Wow. You're quite a renegade attorney. How do I get you out of my life?"

"The hearing is next week and a receiver will be appointed."

"Wow. Then what?"

"Then you can take over the company or sell everything. You can market and sell right? Maybe you feel like being a CEO of a med-tech company using all the benefits you brought to the table?"

"That's not an exit strategy. I haven't done that before."

"Could be worth thinking about. You could probably do anything now."

"What's the downside? "

"They could file for bankruptcy."

"Then?"

"It's not what it used to be. It's much harder now. The court doesn't automatically accept it. If it does, it could be the same result. The court also seizes and sells assets or you could get a shot at restructuring the company. Their best option always was to make a deal with you."

"Holy crap." She hung up and sat for a moment. She shrugged and went back to rummaging in her purse.

"Look," Lena said to the woman next to her as she pulled out a card. "My AARP card. All's right with the world now. Life really does begin at 50, you know." The woman hugged Lena. Lena made a face and pulled at her shirt. She looked down at a mushed berry in her bra.

In the office bathroom cleaning her grey-looking bra, Lena looked confidently at her reflection in the mirror. She held up her hands in a lowered goal post signal with only index fingers pointing up for emphasis and twisted from side to side, "My name is Le-na, I'm FIF-TY, I'm a REA-L-TOR! And I have arrived!" She exited the bathroom, then the office. She said goodbye in Spanglish as she walked out the door. She got in her car that was ridiculously parked, cranked up the radio, and drove off singing loudly to the Rolling Stones – "You can't always get what you want...."

99

Later that day, Lena met her father, Lori, and Kevin at a deli. It was a big night out. Over pickles, Lena and her father ate quietly. She looked around the table. George still looked a little tired, weak, and droopy. Lori pushed her food around. Kevin hit himself in the face with his fork, leaving food on his cheek and him confused. Lena knew she still wasn't in the best of shape either.

After a moment, George stopped eating. He looked at her with a full mouth and piece of pickle on his lips. "It's all about the choices," he said holding the rest of the pickle and using it to emphasize his point. "It's good to have them and great to make them." Lena picked up a pickle and bit it. Her father looked at her, nodded, looked back at his plate, and resumed eating. A few moments passed. "Pass the bread dear." Lena did as she was told. And smiled.

www.ingramcontent.com/pod-product-compliance
Lightning Source LLC
Chambersburg PA
CBHW072221170626
46813CB00003B/1041